SECURING BRENAE

SEAL of Protection: Legacy, Book 1.5

SUSAN STOKER

CHAPTER ONE

T*hirty-One Years Ago*
Annapolis, MD

Brenae Goldner leaned her ass against the countertop in the kitchen of the diner she worked at and closed her eyes. Her day had already been long and tiring before the group of Naval Academy midshipmen had arrived. After forty-five minutes of trying to keep herself out of the way of their roaming hands and listening to their crude pick-up lines and innuendos, she was completely done with today.

All she wanted to do was go back to her tiny little studio apartment and sleep. But after her shift at the diner she had to study for her accounting exam the next day. She was in her second year at the local community college and would be graduating with her Associate's Degree in Business at the end of the year.

If she was being honest, all she really wanted to do with her life was be a wife and mother, but that wouldn't exactly pay the bills. And since she didn't even have a boyfriend, that goal seemed a long ways off.

"You all right, Brenae?" asked Joe, one of the short-order cooks.

She opened her eyes and took a deep breath. "Yeah, just taking a breather," she told him with a smile.

The older man gave her a sympathetic look. "Want me to go out there and knock some heads together?"

Brenae chuckled. "I think I'm good. But thanks."

The serious look Joe gave her made Brenae miss her folks more than she did already. After she'd graduated from high school, they'd decided they'd had enough of the sometimes brutal winters in Maryland and had moved down to Florida. She'd grown apart from her high school girlfriends, and because she went to school and worked so many hours at the diner to pay for her classes, food, rent, and everything else she needed, she didn't have time to go out and make *new* friends.

The stress Brenae was under made her shoulders slump once more. She was tired. Physically and mentally. And the midshipmen she had to go out and deal with weren't helping one bit.

Generally, she didn't mind that the diner was near the US Naval Academy. It meant that business was rarely slow, which made her shifts go by faster and she earned more tips, but it also meant she had to deal with the men and women who were training to be the future leaders in the navy.

Most were kind and pleasant to be around, but there were also those who had no intention of making the navy their career and were only attending the academy because Mom or Dad said they had to or because of some family legacy.

Brenae hated to discriminate or make generalizations about people, but tonight was one of those nights she couldn't help it. The six men at the table were loud, rude, obnoxious, and spoiled. She knew the one who had been the most handsy was named Enzo. Each time he'd put his hand on her arm or ass, his buddies would egg him on. The last time she'd gone out there to take their dessert order, he'd had the audacity to slip his fingers up under her skirt and touch the back of her thigh. Brenae had glared at him and told him to keep his hands to himself, but he'd merely laughed. She had a feeling she was now a challenge to him, and she knew enough to know that wasn't a good thing.

Sighing, she smiled at Joe when she saw he was still eyeballing her. "I'm really okay, Joe. I just need to bring them their dessert, then they'll leave."

"When you're off shift, let me know and I'll escort you to your car."

"Thanks," she told him softly. Joe was older than the other cooks, but he'd always gone out of his way to make sure she felt safe, including walking her the twenty feet from the back door to her car. She always protested, saying it wasn't that far and she'd been fine, but he insisted. Brenae knew he was married with two kids, and she admired his work ethic and the fact that he never ever said anything derogatory about his wife, even in jest. He was one hundred percent devoted to her, and Brenae wanted what he had more than anything in the world.

She was only twenty, but the more time went on, the more she felt as if her opportunity to meet someone who was as devoted to her as Joe was to his wife was slipping away. A lot of people met their significant others in high school or college. And since her late teens, she'd been way too busy studying and working to take the time to go to parties or hang out anywhere else to meet guys.

"Order's up," said Robert, one of the other cooks, motioning to the array of desserts he'd prepared for her table.

"Thanks," she told him with a nod. Break time was over. She walked over and arranged the various plates of sweets on her tray. Taking a deep breath, Brenae lifted the tray and headed out into the diner, praying she could deliver the food and escape without another incident.

Dag Creasy sat at a back table in the diner and watched the pretty waitress as she exited the back of the restaurant and headed for the table of assholes she'd been waiting on for the last hour or so. He was supposed to be studying, and had decided a change in venue would help him. He was in his third year at the Naval Academy and couldn't wait to graduate and start on his lifelong dream of being an officer.

But he couldn't concentrate because the assholes nearby were being overly obnoxious and disrespectful to their waitress. If there was one thing Dag couldn't stand, it was people being rude to others. Especially when being rude involved sexually harassing someone. He'd been keeping his eye on the waitress, and the last time she'd been to the other table, a guy who was in a class below him named Enzo'd had the nerve to slide his hand up the back of her skirt.

Dag had been halfway out of his chair when the waitress had quickly stepped away from Enzo, glared at him, and walked into the kitchen with their order.

Enzo was a bully. There was no other way to describe him. He didn't give a shit about the navy or the academy. Rumor had it he was there only because his parents forced him to attend. He was smart, had to be in order to get in, but he was an asshole.

His studying forgotten, Dag watched as the waitress cautiously approached the table with a tray loaded down with desserts. He was glad to see she stayed away from Enzo as she began to distribute the various plates. But eventually she had to get near him to serve his dessert—and just as he had the last time she was there, he slipped his hand up the back of her skirt.

But this time the waitress couldn't back away

from him because he'd latched onto her thigh with his hand, preventing her from escaping.

Dag couldn't stop himself from moving. He was out of his seat and halfway across the diner before he could talk himself out of it. If the waitress had looked like she was enjoying Enzo's hand on her or his flirting, he would've minded his own business. But the scared look on her face and the way she winced when his fingers dug into her skin made it impossible for him to sit back and do nothing.

He approached the underclassman and, without a word, reached out and grabbed his arm, squeezing a pressure point and forcing Enzo to drop his hand from the waitress's leg.

"Ow, what the fuck?" Enzo complained.

"Did she *ask* you to touch her?" Dag asked. To his surprise, instead of fleeing to the back, the waitress stepped closer to him. They weren't touching, but he could practically feel her body heat against his side and back.

"Not with words, but with her eyes," Enzo said, trying to pull his arm from Dag's grasp, with no luck.

"I did not," the waitress fired back. "In fact, I told you several times to keep your hands to yourself!"

Dag liked her spunk, but he didn't like the quiver

he could hear in her voice, as if she was only pretending to be tough.

"So she told you to fuck off and you still put your hands on her?" Dag asked in a low, deadly tone.

"I thought she was playing hard to get," Enzo mumbled.

Dag knew he was lying. Even from across the room, he could read the "stay away" vibes the waitress had been putting off.

"Are you all even supposed to be eating that shit?" he asked, changing the focus of his anger to the entire table of midshipmen. There were strict rules for them, and since the men at this table were only in their second year, they had more rigorous rules than the upperclassmen did. Including what they shouldn't be eating—namely, the gluttonous desserts currently on their table.

Dag had a good reputation at the academy, and he knew, as did the assholes at the table, that he was in line to become a brigade commander the next year. Someone who was chosen for outstanding leadership performance and was in charge of the brigade's day-to-day activities and the training of other midshipmen. Basically, class president. Dag would love to take on that responsibility. In the meantime, he'd be damned if he sat around and let these midshipmen harass and bully the waitress.

"If I were you," he said sternly, "I'd get your asses back to Bancroft Hall and confess in detail how you broke the Honor Concept and volunteer for additional sexual harassment training."

Enzo glared at him, while the other midshipmen's eyes widened in dismay. They knew better than to defy him. They all knew he could make their lives miserable at the academy.

Dag let go of Enzo's arm and took a step back, making sure to keep himself between the waitress and the table. "And don't forget to leave your waitress a twenty percent tip," he added as the men gathered up their things. There wasn't much free time at the academy, but the study hours from eight to eleven each night were a chance for the midshipmen to take a break from the everyday monotony by escaping for a while. Dag knew he'd be recommending these six men's ability to leave the campus was curtailed for a while.

Without another word, the men slunk out of the small diner into the night and headed back to the dorm.

Dag turned to the waitress. "You okay?"

She nodded.

"I apologize on behalf of those jackals. Not all of us are cut from the same cloth."

She studied him with a look in her eyes he couldn't interpret.

"They seemed almost afraid of you," she said after a moment.

Dag shrugged. "My plan is to make the navy a life-long career. I take every single thing to do with my future very seriously. I've made a name for myself at the academy for being a straight-shooter and a leader."

She nodded and held out a hand. "I'm Brenae. Brenae Goldner."

"Dag Creasy," he said, taking hold of her outstretched hand.

The second their hands touched, Dag felt an almost sharp zing race up his arm and into his chest. They stood there silently for several seconds, clasping hands and staring into each others' eyes.

"It's good to meet you," Brenae said softly.

"Likewise," Dag told her. When he finally loosened his grip on her hand, he felt almost bereft that he had to let her go. The feeling was strange. His entire life, he'd set his sights on becoming a naval officer. Eventually he wanted to be a Navy SEAL. In the upcoming summer, he was taking his summer cruise with Special Warfare and couldn't wait to see firsthand how the SEALs operated.

But all of a sudden, and for the first time, he was dreading spending the time away from Annapolis.

"I get off shift in twenty minutes," Brenae said shyly. "Any chance you'd like to have a cup of coffee with me?"

"Absolutely." He liked that Brenae wasn't afraid to ask him out.

Okay, they weren't actually going out on a date... but he could pretend.

She nodded at him, then backed away, only breaking eye contact at the last minute when she had to turn and head back through the door leading into the kitchen.

Brenae had no idea what she was dong. This wasn't like her. She wasn't forward like this. But there was something about Dag that had her acting out of character.

Everything about the man who'd come to her rescue appealed to her. His hair was closely cropped, as was the hair of all the guys who went to the academy. He had brown eyes and she loved how tall he was. She could tell he was muscular and strong by the way he'd easily controlled Enzo. She definitely liked how sure he was about what he wanted to do with his life.

It might be a mistake to get involved with a navy man, she knew he didn't have a lot of time to do anything other than the activities planned by the academy, but she couldn't help herself.

She hurried through the last of the things she needed to do in order to go off shift and wished she was wearing something other than the cheesy diner uniform as she wandered back into the dining room.

Dag stood as she approached, which made her smile. He certainly had good manners, and that went a long way in her eyes. So many guys today were only interested in a good time, they didn't even think about things like opening doors, saying please and thank you, and generally just being respectful.

"Hi," she said as she approached him.

"Hi," he returned, then gestured to the seat across from him.

Brenae slipped into it—and felt awkward all of a sudden. What was she doing? She didn't know this guy. Just because he'd stood up for her and was gorgeous didn't mean he was interested in her in any way. Maybe he was just humoring her. She hadn't really given him much choice but to agree to her stupid offer for coffee, what with being a ridiculous "damsel in distress" and all. And shit, she'd forgotten to even *bring* them coffee.

"Stop worrying," he said gently as he settled himself in the seat across from her.

She bit her lip, then asked, "How did you know I was stressing?"

"I can just tell. I wouldn't have agreed to coffee if I didn't want to."

Mentally sighing in relief, Brenae nodded. "Some waitress I am, I forgot to even bring us drinks."

Dag shrugged. "It's okay. I really only wanted to spend some time getting to know you."

"Why?" The question popped out before she could call it back. Brenae knew she was blushing, but couldn't stop it.

Dag chuckled. "I like that you say what you're thinking."

"It gets me in trouble more often than not," she admitted.

"But it's real. And I admire that. And to answer your question, you caught my eye the second I came in tonight. And not to freak you out or anything, but I watched how you dealt with Enzo and his buddies all night, and until he'd decided to put his hands on you, I was impressed at how you stayed friendly, but kept a professional distance with them at the same time."

"Thanks."

"That happen a lot?"

"What?"

"Assholes thinking it's okay to touch you without your permission?"

Brenae shrugged. "It kind of comes with the job."

"No," Dag said firmly. "Fuck that. No one gets to touch you if you don't want them too."

She blinked at the vehemence in his voice. "It's not a big deal, Dag. Most of the time it's just them touching my hand, or maybe my leg...*over* my skirt."

Dag leaned forward, and she couldn't look away from the intensity in his gaze. "Wrong. It's not okay. It's *never* okay. And you shouldn't let anyone talk to you or touch you in a way you aren't comfortable with. It's disrespectful as hell and harassment."

Brenae thought about it for only a second before realizing he was right, of course. She'd kinda just taken the harassment as coming with the job, part of being a waitress, but honestly, if someone had put their hands on her like Enzo had before she'd started working at the diner, she would've lost her shit. Just because she was in a service job didn't mean she had to put up with that kind of thing. "You're right."

Dag took a deep breath and sat back. They stared at each other for a long moment before she asked, "So...you want to be a naval officer?" she asked.

Dag smiled—and it took her breath away. He was good-looking when he was all broody and serious, but when he grinned, he was gorgeous.

"Yeah. One day in elementary school, a Navy SEAL came to our class and talked to us about what it was he did, and from that day forth that's all I've wanted to do."

"A SEAL, huh?" Brenae asked.

He nodded. "That's the ultimate goal. I know it won't be easy. It'll be brutally hard, in fact, but I can do it."

She liked his confidence. She huffed out a short laugh. "I should be graduating with my two-year degree in business this spring and I have no idea what I want to do with my life."

"I have a feeling you'll be good at whatever you decide to do," Dag said.

Brenae rolled her eyes. "You don't even know me."

"I'm trying to rectify that," he said smoothly.

For the next hour, they talked about everything from their parents to where their dream vacation would be. Brenae told him about how she had never really seen much of the world other than the Baltimore area, and he told her more about SEAL training.

She looked down at her watch and grimaced.

"What?" he asked.

"I hate to do this, and it's not a line, but I really need to go home and study. I have an accounting test tomorrow and I can't afford to fail it."

Dag immediately nodded and began to pack up his stuff.

"Oh, but I didn't mean you had to leave," she told him.

He stopped and looked her in the eyes once more. She loved how he did that. He didn't shy away from making that intimate connection with her. "It's about time for me to go as well. I need to get back and report Enzo, and curfew is coming up. But I'd like to see you again, Brenae."

Butterflies swirled around in her stomach. She'd been hoping he might ask her out, on a real date this time, but hadn't wanted to get her hopes up too high. "I'd like that."

He smiled. "But first, I'm going to walk you to your car. You need to grab anything before you go?"

"No, I've got my purse. I'm good."

Dag stood, and when she stumbled getting out of the booth, he was right there with a hand at her elbow. "Thanks. We can go out the back door. My car's in the lot behind the diner."

As they walked through the diner, she was well aware of Dag's hand at her back. He wasn't pushing her, wasn't really touching her much at all. At most, his fingertips brushed against the small of her back as they walked, but she was aware of every brush of his hand on her body. Goose bumps broke out...and crazy as it was, Brenae suspected she was already falling hard and fast for the man beside her.

They went out into the dark night, and Brenae shivered.

"Cold?" he asked in concern.

"I'll be good until I can get the heat in my car cranked up," she replied.

She led him over to her car and turned to him shyly once they were there.

Dag's gaze swept her from head to toe, surprisingly not lingering at her boobs. It was more an assessing look, making sure she was all right, rather than a leering one.

"Do you have far to go?" he asked.

Brenae shook her head. "Not too far. Only about ten minutes or so."

He nodded. Then said something that surprised her. "I'm going to be a career navy guy. And you know I'm trying to be a SEAL. That means lots of deployments. I could be gone for two weeks at a time, or twelve *months* at a time. I won't be able to predict it."

Brenae frowned in confusion. "Okaaaaay...?"

He held out his hand, and she automatically put hers in it. His fingers closed around hers and he brought her hand up to his mouth and kissed the back. "I'm telling you this because I'm interested in you, Brenae. You intrigue me, and you make me feel things I haven't ever felt about someone before. And if I feel this way after talking to you for just an hour, I have a suspicion those feelings will only get stronger the more I get to know you. If things between us work out the way I'm hoping they do... well, that means what I do with my life will affect you too. So I'm telling you now what will happen in my career to make sure you'll be able to handle it."

Brenae blinked up at him, heart pounding.

Holy crap. She didn't know whether to be freaked out that he wanted a long-term relationship with her, after only knowing her an hour, or to be excited and giddy.

The latter won out.

"I can handle it," she told him.

"Don't be so quick to answer. It means that you'll be alone a lot. And if we get married and have kids someday, you'll have to shoulder much of the responsibility simply because I'm not there to do my part. Don't get me wrong, when I *am* home, I'll be one hundred percent invested, but there'll be times when my future wife will have to deal with the toilet overflowing, one of the kids having to go to the emergency room for a broken bone, and a thousand other little things on her own because I'm not there."

Brenae wasn't sure if he was trying to warn her away from him or what, but at the mention of having children with this man, all she could think of was the *making* of said imaginary kids—and how amazing she was sure that would be.

"I'm getting a business degree because I love learning, and it was the one major I thought could be adaptable to almost anything I decided to do. But to be frank, I'd like nothing more than to be a full-time mother. I know that's not a popular choice in today's world of women's lib, but...it's truly how I feel. And I have no problem with you being deployed. I want any man I'm with to do what they feel passionate about. And how could I ever get upset with you for wanting to serve your country?"

His face gentled, and for the first time, she saw passion in his eyes. She licked her lips—and couldn't take her eyes from his. His fingers tightened on her hand.

"I'd like to kiss you," he said quietly.

He didn't lean forward. Didn't pressure her in any way.

Once more, he was showing her that he was a true gentleman, and it made her fall for him all the more.

"I'd like that," she returned softly.

Then Dag moved slowly. His free hand came up to the back of her neck and gently caressed her with his thumb, even as he brought their clasped hands around to her back. Brenae grabbed onto his biceps with her free hand and practically held her breath as he unhurriedly bent toward her.

Just before his lips touched hers, Dag said, "I have a feeling I'm going to remember this kiss for the rest of my life."

His warm breath wafted over her before he finally kissed her.

Brenae closed her eyes and clutched at his arm

as Dag took control of the kiss. He nibbled and teased her lips with his teeth and tongue before she groaned low in her throat. Taking that as consent, or for the impatience it was meant to be, she felt him smile against her before he slanted his head and took what they both wanted...and needed.

The kiss was nothing like anything Brenae had experienced before. Dag overwhelmed her senses. Her eyes closed and she could smell what she assumed was the soap he'd used the last time he'd showered. She felt his fingers tighten sensually against the back of her neck. He didn't press her against her car, didn't shove his crotch against her, try to crudely show her how much she turned him on. His tongue simply caressed hers over and over, and it somehow felt as if this was her first kiss.

A part of her knew, deep down, that Dag would be the one and only person she ever kissed this way.

When he finally pulled away, he only backed off enough to look her into her eyes.

Instinctively, Brenae knew her life had just changed. Irrevocably and for the better. Life as a military spouse wouldn't be easy, especially with a take-charge man like Dag. But she suddenly couldn't imagine doing anything else with her life. With him at her side, she could accomplish anything. Go anywhere. Be anyone she wanted.

"Holy fuck," he said softly.

Brenae smiled. Huge. His words were crass, but she couldn't have said it better herself.

He seemed to gather himself and took a deep breath. She watched as he licked his lips sensuously.

Without thought, she stood up on her tiptoes and kissed him gently. It was a closed-mouth kiss this time, and even more romantic and tender as a result.

"Not that I'm complaining, but what was that one for?" he asked.

"I just...I wanted to taste you one last time." She felt stupid the second the words left her lips, but the way he smiled down at her took away any embarrassment she might've felt about her impulsive act.

"Give me your number," he ordered.

"Do you need to write it down?" she asked.

Dag didn't move away from her. "No, I'll remember it."

She rattled it off, and he repeated it back to her. "I'll call you tomorrow night. Are you working? What time do you get off?"

"Same time."

"Okay. I can't come to the diner tomorrow, but I'll

call you to make sure you got home all right."

"I'd like that."

"You don't have to worry about Enzo and his buddies coming to the diner again. I'm going to make sure he knows it's off limits from here on out."

"I can handle him," Brenae said.

"I know you can. But now you don't have to. I probably shouldn't say this right now, because it could work against me. But I'm overprotective. Always have been, always will be. When you're with me, I'm going to do my best to make sure that you're safe. And even when I'm not around, I'll still do what I can to make your life easier, as much as possible. Got it?"

Brenae shivered and nodded.

Misinterpreting her shiver and thinking she was chilly, Dag said, "I'm an idiot for making you stand out here in the cold in that dress. Drive safe getting home, and I'll talk to you tomorrow."

Brenae nodded, feeling slightly disappointed when he took his hands off her and helped her into her car. She rolled down the window and called, "Dag?"

"Yeah, Brea?"

Loving the way he said her name, she said, "For the record, I'm proud of you. Not everyone is made for serving their country, and even only knowing you for the short time that I have, I know you're going to make an excellent Officer and SEAL. Our country is lucky to have you on their side."

"Thank you. That means the world to me. Later, Brea."

"Later, Dag."

Brenae drove back to her small studio apartment, a huge smile on her face the entire way. It was amazing how one minute she was depressed and lonely, and the next she felt as if she had a whole new life ahead of her. Ultimately, she had no idea if things with Dag would actually work out...but she had a really good feeling about it. About *them*.

That night, she had a dream. She and Dag both had gray hair and were sitting on a love seat on the back deck of a big house on a beach. They were watching the sunset and were holding hands, simply sitting with each other and enjoying the romantic setting.

Dag turned to her and said, "I'm the luckiest man alive. Who would've thought all those years ago that we'd be here today?"

And dream-Brenae turned to her husband, the man she'd loved for what felt like her entire life, and said, "Me."

CHAPTER TWO

resent Day
     Riverton, CA

Brenae Creasy sat on the rock wall on the beach and tried to be patient. When she and her husband, Rear Admiral Dag Creasy, had arrived at the quarterly SEAL family picnic earlier, their plans had been to hang around just long enough to say hello to the men under his command, and then head back home.

Home at the moment was an apartment, as the house they were having built wasn't ready yet. Their other house had sold surprisingly fast, and thus, they were marking time in an apartment for a few months until they could move into their dream home overlooking the Pacific Ocean.

But not too long after they'd arrived at the beach, their lazy day out had taken a turn. The traitor her husband had been looking for had made his move and tried to kill a young woman right there on the beach.

Brenae had watched the whole thing in disbelief and fear, both for her husband and the woman who had almost died. Without blinking, Dag had entered the fray right along with the much younger Navy SEALs. When shots had rung out over the beach, shattering the peaceful and fun outing, she still hadn't panicked. She trusted Dag, and more importantly, she trusted the SEALs he worked with.

More than two hours had passed since the incident, but Brenae refused to leave. Dag had come over and spoken to her briefly, telling her he was going to be a while and she should go on home, but she'd declined. She'd done what she could to reassure the other wives and their children before they'd left, but even when the air cooled and she shivered, she refused to budge.

Dag was stressed. She'd been married to the man for almost thirty years. She could read him better than anyone in the world. To everyone else, he was the one they turned to for direction. They looked up to him and respected him...almost revered him. But to her, he was just Dag. The two of them had been through so much. She knew him inside and out. And right now, he was hurting. She wasn't leaving without him. No way.

Brenae had always been proud of Dag, but at that moment, watching how easily he handled everyone around him, reassuring those who needed it, using his rank to smooth things over with law enforcement, and being compassionate to the young woman who had almost lost her life that evening... she was even more proud.

Every time she looked at her husband, she saw the young sailor she'd met when he was at the Naval Academy and she was a struggling community college student working at a rundown diner. But it was times like this when it was hammered home that he was one hell of a leader. Men and women looked up to him, looked *to* him, when the shit hit the fan.

By the time the sun started sinking below the horizon, most of the police officers and naval investigators had left the beach. The SEALs who'd been directly involved in the rescue of the woman had been dismissed.

Brenae watched as Dag finally shook the hands of the remaining law enforcement personnel and made his way toward her. He was wearing a pair of jeans and a black T-shirt, but even out of uniform, he had no problem garnishing respect from everyone he met. But Brenae couldn't take her eyes off his face.

He was exhausted. And sad. And pissed. And worried—about her. She hated adding to his worries, but there was no way she could've left. She stood when he approached, and to her surprise, instead of putting his hand on her back and leading her to their car, he reached out and enfolded her in his arms instead.

Dag wasn't a demonstrative man. Especially in public. He was always aware of his rank and the responsibilities that came with it. As a career navy man, he'd learned a long time ago to hide his true feelings behind a stoic mask. So taking her in his arms and holding on as if she was a feather who would blow away in a brisk breeze was an unusual move, and made her heart clench.

She was half a foot shorter than his six feet, but she still felt him bury his nose in her hair as he held on to her. Wrapping her own arms around the man she loved with all her being, Brenae palmed the back of his head, the short hair brushing against her palm in a way that was familiar and comforting.

"I'm sorry," she said softly. "That had to have sucked."

"Yeah," Dag mumbled against her hair.

"You're okay, right?" she asked.

He huffed out a small chuckle and straightened and looked down at her. "I thought you'd grown out of asking me that."

Brenae mock glared up at her husband. "Dag, you came home from a mission with a *bullet wound* and tried to blow it off as if it was nothing."

He shrugged. "I hadn't seen you in a month. The scratch on my arm could wait. Seeing you couldn't."

She melted inside at his words, but still scowled at him. "Scratch? The bullet was still inside your arm! *And* it was infected." She shook her head at him. "I learned my lesson that day. Make sure you're really okay first, *then* carry on with whatever we were going to do."

"I'm okay, hon. Promise," he said softly, his brown eyes fixed on hers.

"Good. You're cleared to leave?"

"Yeah. The navy is sending someone over to notify his wife of his death."

"We should go over tomorrow."

Dag swallowed hard before nodding. "I wasn't going to assume you'd want to go with me."

"I've known *her* for as long as you knew him. This is going to be hard for her and their kids."

"I know. I love you, Brenae. I don't know what the hell you saw in me when I was a punk-ass kid, but I've never regretted one day of the time we've spent together."

"Me either," Brenae told him. Their marriage had certainly had its ups and downs. Thirty years of being married to a man devoted to the military wasn't a walk in the park, but when all was said and done, she'd never stopped loving him. "Let's go home."

"God, I wish our house was done," he mumbled. "There's nothing more I'd like than a nice long soak in that hot tub being installed on our deck."

Brenae agreed with him, but simply said, "We'll make do with a shower. Come on."

Dag put his arm around her waist and hugged her to his side as he walked them to their car in the parking lot. It was one of the last ones in the deserted lot, but he still constantly looked around, making sure she was safe as they walked toward it.

Within fifteen minutes, they were pulling up to their apartment complex. It was dark by then, and again, Dag made sure to keep an eye out for trouble as he led her to the front doors. One of the things Brenae loved about her husband was the way he constantly touched her when they were alone. In public he was always the consummate professional, always aware that people were watching him, judging him. But in private, he more than made up for his lack of public displays of affection. If they were close enough to touch...he did. His fingers at the small of her back. A hand on her arm. His hand engulfing hers.

It was a short ride up to the third floor and before she knew it, they were inside their two-bedroom apartment.

The second the door closed behind them, Dag took her hand in his and made a beeline for their bedroom.

Surprised, Brenae followed him without a word. She was hungry, as they'd been on the beach for hours, but she didn't complain. Whatever Dag needed right now, she'd gladly provide for him.

He headed straight for the bathroom attached to their master bedroom. It wasn't anything special, Formica countertops, the walls a putrid green color. But since it was a rental, it wasn't like she was going to spend the money or time to remodel. Dag held on to her hand even as he leaned over and turned on the water in the shower. Then he stood and looked her in the eyes as he finally dropped her hand and began stripping.

Brenae couldn't help but stare at her husband. At fifty-three, he was still just as handsome as he'd been at twenty-one. More so, actually. He'd lost his boyish hotness and now looked distinguished. His brown hair was turning silver and the scruff of his beard was gray rather than the dark brown it used to be. He had lines on either side of his eyes, but the look in them was just as intense now as it had been when he was in college.

He tugged off his shirt and Brenae licked her lips in anticipation. His biceps bulged with his movements, and she loved the prominent the veins in his forearms.

He couldn't quite keep up with the SEALs who trained on the beach every morning anymore, but he wasn't exactly ready for the nursing home, either. His stomach was still flat, and he still had the faint outline of a six-pack there. He was so incredibly handsome...and he was all hers.

"You gonna join me?" Dag asked softly as he pushed his jeans down his muscular thighs. The bulge in his boxer briefs could still make her mouth water in anticipation. Her man might be in his fifties, but damn, he was so fucking hot, sometimes Brenae still had a hard time believing he was with her.

Dag had been her first and only lover, and she'd never felt as if she'd missed out on anything. He'd always made sure she was satisfied before he took his own pleasure. Every single time. Dag was a generous lover, and inventive too.

When he shoved his underwear down his legs, Brenae licked her lips again and shook herself out of the trance she'd been in. Removing her own clothes in record time, she was soon as naked as her husband. She was showing her age a bit more than she was comfortable with, but Dag's eyes never failed to sparkle when he saw her naked, and that was all she cared about.

He held out a hand to steady her as she stepped over the rim of the bathtub into the generic shower, much too small for her liking. Dag joined her immediately. Reaching for the water, he turned it just a bit hotter, then sat down at the bottom of the tub.

Knowing what he needed, Brenae turned her back to the water, and straddled her husband's thighs. The second she was seated upon him, his knees came up, pressing her into his chest and cocooning them in the bottom of the tub, the air quickly filling with steam. Brenae wrapped her arms around Dag's neck and buried her nose into the space between his neck and shoulder. She felt his arms clamp around her as well. One around her waist, keeping her steady, and the other around her upper back.

It wasn't often Dag wanted to cuddle like this. But in the privacy of their home, the steam so thick around them it was hard to even see each other, he let down his guard. With her. Only with her.

Brenae felt his chest heave with the first sob, and her arms tightened. Tears fell from her own eyes as she held her big tough Navy SEAL while he cried. Cried because the person he'd thought was his friend, someone he'd respected, had turned against his government and had tried to murder someone. He'd let greed take over his life and change him into a man Dag didn't know anymore.

Brenae knew tomorrow, her husband would be back to normal. Would be the man everyone looked up to and respected. The man who'd stand face to face with his friend's widow and let her blame *him* if she needed to. But here in their little corner of the world, Dag was a man who needed the loving embrace of his wife.

CHAPTER THREE

Rear Admiral Dag Creasy woke up in the middle of the night and turned to look at his wife. The last week had sucked, but Brenae handled it like she always did. From holding his friend's widow as she cried, to organizing with the other spouses to make sure there was food in her freezer, to ensuring her children were getting counseling.

Dag knew being married to him wasn't the easiest thing in the world, especially as his rank climbed. When he'd met Brenae, she'd been a naïve waitress trying to make it through community college. Neither of them would've ever guessed thirty years later, she'd be hobnobbing with the highest-ranking officers in the US Navy. She'd even met the First Lady of the United States when the

President had come into town for some political thing.

But the thing he loved most about his wife was how she'd never lost her down-to-earth qualities. She was the one person he could truly be himself with. He could prop his feet on their coffee table, drink beer, and burp to his heart's content as he watched Sunday night football, and she wouldn't even blink.

She was his rock.

The one person who he knew without a doubt would be there for him no matter what.

When he'd injured his leg on a mission when he'd been a SEAL, Brenae had been the one who'd pulled his head out of his ass and made him get into physical therapy. If it hadn't been for her browbeating, he might still be in a wheelchair today. When he'd hit rock bottom, suffering from PTSD and feeling depressed over his injury, and he'd tried to make her hate him, she'd seen through his bravado, climbed into their bed late at night, and simply held him. She'd told him over and over how much she loved him, and it didn't matter if he never walked again, she wasn't ever going to leave him. He was stuck with her.

A week ago, after he'd watched a man he'd liked

and respected shoot himself in the head, she'd once again been his savior. She'd refused to leave the beach, and every time he'd looked over and seen her patiently waiting for him, sitting on the hard rock wall as if she'd wait there all night if she had to, it had grounded him. Helped him get through one of the worst evenings he'd had in a very long time.

Then she'd taken him into her arms in their crappy apartment shower and held him as he'd wept. She never judged him. She took him as he was, and he loved her more than life itself.

It was early, the light from the full moon still bright as it shone through the thin piece-of-shit curtains in the master bedroom. Dag scowled, deciding to put more pressure on the contractor to get their fucking house finished faster. They'd done their time living in tiny apartments. He wanted to give his wife the world, and this apartment just wasn't cutting it.

Slowly, he eased the sheet down until he could see every inch of his wife. He wanted to turn the light on so he could really see her, but honestly, he didn't need the light because he knew every inch of his Brenae's body. At fifty-one, she was just as beautiful to him as she'd been at nineteen. Her light brown hair was the same color as it'd been the day they got married...thanks to the hair stylist she went to every other month. She had stretch marks on her belly from carrying their two children, and he knew she thought her thighs and butt were too big and her tits sagged too much.

But he loved every fucking inch of her. She was his. The one thing that gotten him through the darkest of missions when he'd been a SEAL. She was the reason he did what he did...to make her proud of him. She was his light. His everything.

The air in the room was cool because Brenae hated being hot when she slept. He watched as her nipples tightened into hard little buds as they were exposed to the chilly air. He couldn't wait until they were in their new house with the giant ceiling fan above their four-poster bed, which was currently in storage. He'd worked hard to give Brenae the material things she deserved. But the thing about his wife was, Dag knew that while she enjoyed the shoes, jewelry, and nice furniture he'd been able to give to her, ultimately, she didn't give a shit about any of it.

Being here in this small apartment didn't faze her, as long as they were together.

Leaning over, Dag took one of her tits into his hand, plumping it, and then wrapped his lips around one turgid little nipple. He smiled against her flesh when he felt one of her hands cup the back of his head and hold him to her.

"What time is it?" she whispered.

Lifting his head just enough to answer, Dag said, "Early."

"You didn't get enough last night?" she asked with a small groan.

"I'll never get enough of you," Dag told her honestly. His stamina had lessened over the years, but all that meant was that he could spend more time loving his wife. The days of him being able to fuck her twice in a row were gone, but that didn't mean *Brenae* couldn't come more than once.

Knowing she was awake now, Dag straddled his wife and hovered over her. His cock was at half-mast and brushed against her trimmed pubic hair. He wasn't concerned with the state of his dick. When it was time to enter her, he'd be more than ready. The highlight of his life was feeling Brenae come under his tongue or fingers, and feeling how hot and wet she was when he finally slid inside her welcoming depths.

The memory of the first time he'd taken her— and had found out she was a virgin—was something he'd never forget. She'd trusted him with her body then, and she'd shown over and over again since that she trusted him with whatever he needed or wanted from her. It was humbling at the same time it was intoxicating, and to this day, even a little scary.

"I don't think I said thank you for last week," he told her, looking into her eyes. He knew they were a beautiful blue, but in the dim light of the room, he couldn't make out anything but their shape.

"You don't have to thank me," she assured him.

"I do," Dag said softly. "You always let me be who I am. Whether that's a rear admiral, someone who just wants to goof off, or a broken man."

"You weren't broken," Brenae said immediately. "You're the strongest man I've ever met. But you can't always be strong. When you've reached the end of your rope, that's where I come in. I'll wrap my hands around yours and help you hang on until you can start climbing again."

Dag swallowed hard. How he'd gotten so lucky, he'd never know. Brenae had raised their son and daughter practically by herself. He'd been gone on so many missions, he couldn't even keep track. But Brenae hadn't complained. Not once. She'd just done what needed doing. Just as she'd done when he'd gotten hurt. And when the politics of being his wife caught up to her, and she was the brunt of malicious gossip from other jealous officer wives, she'd held her head up and refused to let them get to her. She was beautiful, gracious, and so fucking strong, she humbled him. He never felt embarrassed or guilty for crying. Not when he could do so in her arms. She held him so tightly, he knew everything was going to be all right.

Knowing he couldn't speak or he'd risk embarrassing himself, Dag moved down her body and settled between her legs. He smiled when she propped herself up with pillows behind her back. She liked to watch him eat her out. Once telling him that seeing how much *he* enjoyed it made her embarrassment over the act, wane.

Dag started by kissing Brenae's inner thigh gently. Then licking where his lips had touched. She squirmed and he grinned, loving that he could so easily turn her on. He nibbled on her flesh for a while, before moving up to the crease of her leg. She widened her thighs and he couldn't help but move his attentions between her legs.

Using his fingers to spread her lower lips apart, he dropped his head. He started out slow, gently licking and caressing her. But it wasn't long before she moaned.

"Dag, stop teasing me."

"I'm not teasing," he said, looking up at her while using his fingers to lightly caress her. "It's foreplay."

"You're driving me crazy and you know it. Please. Lick my clit."

Smiling, Dag lowered his head. He loved how impatient Brenae was. She used to be so shy. Never asking for what she wanted. He'd taught her everything there was to know about sex, and he couldn't help but be proud of the sensual woman she was today. She wasn't afraid to tell him she wasn't in the mood, but she also was more than happy being the aggressor when she was feeling horny. And he loved that they both still enjoyed sex thirty years after they'd gotten married. Many couples, regardless of their age, weren't so lucky.

He felt her hands cup his head. His hair was too short for her to get a good grip, but she did her best to try to shove him where she wanted him. Laughing, Dag let her steer him to her clit. It was exactly where he wanted to be anyway. Loved feeling how hard the little nub got and how it peeked out from beneath the protective hood when she was particularly turned on.

Brenae squirmed under him when he eased a finger into her body as he teased her clit.

"God, Dag, that feels so good," she said huskily.

His mouth was busy, so he couldn't reply, but it felt amazing to him too.

Suddenly wanting to be inside his wife more than he wanted anything else, Dag lifted his head and brought his other hand up to her clit. Using her own juices to lubricate his thumb, he blew cool air over her pussy as he added a finger inside her sheath and began to manipulate her clit with his thumb.

"God! Dag!" Brenae exclaimed, and her hips came up off the bed as he finger-fucked her.

"So beautiful," he murmured as he watched her writhe under his hands.

They might've had their issues as a married couple, but not once had he ever had the urge to take someone else to his bed. Only Brenae could turn him on. Only Brenae could satisfy him.

Her head tilted back, and she let go of his head to reach for the sheets. Her hands fisted and she groaned long and low as every muscle in her body tensed.

Dag groaned right along with her; he knew first-hand how those tense muscles felt around his dick when she came with him deep inside her.

Moving quickly, he got up on his knees and physically picked up Brenae and turned her onto her stomach. He lifted her hips high into the air and pushed his hard cock inside her still spasming sheath.

Brenae gasped as she got up on her hands, but pushed back against him when he pulled her toward him. Holding her still, making her take just what he wanted to give her, Dag pressed back inside her. Looking down, he could just make out her juices coating his dick, making it shiny in the dim light.

Putting a hand on her back, he urged her down. Immediately acquiescing, she turned her head so her cheek was on the sheet. She moved her arms down to her sides and beneath her, just as he knew she'd do, and he felt her fingers brushing against his dick as he pulled out. She caressed his balls even as she lazily fingered her clit with her other hand.

This was one of their favorite positions. She could get herself off, fondle him, and he could reach her tits at the same time. He leaned over her, bracing himself on one hand while the other pinched a nipple. They both groaned and her hand tightened on his balls. If he had his way, he'd still be fucking his wife this way when they were both in their eighties. He'd never get enough of her. Never.

Knowing he wasn't going to last long, as he could already feel the slight tingle in his balls, Dag asked, "You ready?"

"Fuck me, Dag," Brenae said in response.

He was upset that he couldn't fuck her for as long as he used to when he was younger, but she swore it was a compliment that he couldn't hold out longer than a few minutes when he finally got inside her.

He got back up on his knees and held his wife's hips and began to fuck her in earnest. She grunted every time he bottomed out inside her, and he could feel her fingers flicking rapidly over her clit as he pumped in and out.

Within fifteen seconds, he knew he was going to come. Doing what he knew would make her explode, he swiped his middle finger through the copious juices coming from her slit and gently pressed against her asshole. He didn't penetrate her, merely caressed the sensitive nerves of her backside.

She shouted in ecstasy, and once again every muscle in her body tensed. It felt as if she was going to squeeze his dick right off, and it was glorious. Grunting, Dag slammed inside her once more and held her to him as he exploded. Spurts of come pulsed out of his dick and coated her inner channel. Even though he knew he couldn't get her pregnant, as he'd gotten a vasectomy years ago, Dag couldn't help but picture his little swimmers frantically trying to find an egg to impregnate.

Her muscles twitched around his cock, prolonging his pleasure and making Dag thank his lucky stars once more for his beautiful and loving wife.

He held himself as deep inside her as he could for several moments, loving how their combined juices almost felt scalding around his sensitive cock. Knowing she had to be uncomfortable with her ass up in the air and her weight on her shoulder, Dag pulled out. They both groaned at the feeling of him leaving her, and he immediately fell onto his side and pulled Brenae into his arms.

Many men didn't like to cuddle, but Dag wasn't one of them. He fucking loved holding Brenae in his arms. Almost as much as he liked making love with her. She was the other half of his soul, and nothing made his mind settle as much as holding her in his arms. He loved the way she snuggled into him. Loved the way she sighed in contentment. Loved how one of her legs would curl around his calf. And he especially loved when she let him scoot down and use her tits as a pillow. She'd hold him close and he'd let her heart lull him to sleep.

After several minutes of cuddling, she asked sleepily, "What do you have on tap for today?"

"PT. Then a meeting with the base commander about what happened last week and to get an update on his replacement. Then I'm meeting with each of the SEAL teams to answer their questions and to reassure them that they will absolutely be safe when they go overseas on a mission in the interim. I have to go to NCIS and answer questions about the traitor from Bahrain, and to find out if I'll have to testify in *his* hearing. I have a stack of paperwork a mile high I have to try to get through, and then hopefully convince my admin that she doesn't want to quit as a result."

"So a normal day," Brenae quipped.

Dag chuckled. "Pretty much."

"You thought any more about retirement?"

Dag stiffened and propped himself up on an elbow and tried to read her face. The light was too low for him to interpret what she was thinking. "You know all you have to do is say the word and I'm done," he said softly.

"I wasn't hinting," Brenae chided. "I just hate seeing you so stressed. I mean, I know you're pretty much *always* stressed, but the last week has been worse. I wasn't sure if everything that happened had tipped the scales, making you want to get out sooner rather than later."

Dag thought about it for a long moment. Then finally said, "Honestly, everything about that situation sucked, but I feel as if I'm needed even more now. I'm not so conceited to think that no one else can do my job, but with everything else going on, I have a feeling keeping things as normal as possible is the best thing for everyone. SEALs, their families, and my own bosses."

"I agree," Brenae said softly. "I'm so proud of you, Dag."

"As long as you can say that, I'm good. The second that changes, I'm out."

"I'll always be proud of you," she said. "Always."

"I love you."

"I love you too."

"I've still got another hour before I have to get up and get ready for work," Dag told her. "Go back to sleep, baby."

"You too?" she asked sleepily.

"Sure," Dag told her, but he knew he was lying. One of this favorite things in the world was holding her while she slept. He'd never told her, but he loved how easily she fell asleep in his arms. How she innately trusted him to keep her safe no matter what.

The second he felt her deep, even breaths, he leaned over and kissed her forehead. "I swear the next thirty years are going to be easier than the first," he vowed.

CHAPTER FOUR

A week later, Brenae was on the first floor of the apartment complex getting her mail from the mailroom, when the door opened. She turned to see who had entered and stared at the woman in surprise. "Caite?"

The woman looked startled for a moment, then tilted her head to the side and said, "Yeah. I'm sorry, I'm terrible with faces. Have we met?"

Brenae smiled, liking the younger woman immediately. She was old enough to be her mother, if she'd had a daughter when she'd first gotten married, but also, something about Caite spoke to her. She'd taken it upon herself to learn as much as she could about the young woman who'd been the victim on the beach a couple of weeks ago. "Not really. I'm Brenae Creasy. My husband is Rear Admiral Creasy."

Caite immediately blushed. "Oh Lord. I'm so sorry I didn't recognize you! I feel like an idiot. My boyfriend talks about your husband all the time. He admires him so much. And he was there when that crap on the beach went down. I haven't seen him since then, but I wanted to thank him again for all he did."

Brenae waved off Caite's thanks. "He was just doing what he does best."

Caite bit her lip, then said, "I've worked around military people for a while now, and I've learned to watch what I say...especially to spouses. I never know if they're going to take what I say the wrong way or not. And now that I'm dating a SEAL, I'm even more paranoid I'm gonna say the wrong thing, especially to someone who's married to someone as high ranking as your husband. But...I really want to ask something. I just don't know if I should."

Brenae's respect for the young woman rose even more at her honesty. She reminded her a lot of herself twenty-five years ago. She'd tried so hard to fit in, to make friends, only to get stabbed in the back more than once. It wasn't until she'd stopped caring what everyone else thought that she finally came into her own. "Please, be honest. I can't stand people who are nice to me because of who my husband is or any other superficial crap."

"Is your husband okay?" Caite asked.

Brenae blinked. She thought for sure Caite was going to ask what in the world they were doing living in the apartment complex. Or what it was like being married to one of the highest-ranking officers on the base. Or something about the SEALs. The last thing she expected was for her to ask about Dag.

No one ever wondered how her husband coped with stuff that happened, they just assumed he was fine because he'd been a SEAL.

She had to take a second to compose herself before she answered. "He's okay. Thanks."

Caite reached out and put her hand on Brenae's arm. "Seriously, is he really okay? Rocco said he was friends with..." She swallowed hard before continuing. "Anyway, I just wanted to make sure he was doing all right. Rocco didn't *personally* know the guy, so he was just worried about me when the stuff on the beach happened. I didn't even know your husband, and he didn't know me, other than in the scope of the investigation, so everything probably hit him differently."

Brenae covered Caite's hand with her own. She

had a feeling in twenty years, the other woman would be a great wife to her own high-ranking husband and a huge asset to the navy. "He's good. One thing you learn when you're married to a tough-as-nails, alpha Navy SEAL is how to help your man let off steam. You figure out when he needs to be held tightly, and when to back off and let him work through shit on his own. I'm not saying it wasn't a blow, but Dag's okay."

"Thank God. I was worried about him," Caite said. "And you're okay too?"

Brenae chuckled. "I should be asking *you* that."

"I'm more thankful than I can say that Rocco insisted on teaching me how to float a week before everything happened."

"You don't know how to swim?" Brenae asked in surprise.

Caite chuckled. "Nope. But I'm pretty good at floating now."

"Let me guess, Rocco has since taken you for several more lessons."

"Of course he has," Caite told her easily. "But it's not exactly a hardship to see him in his bathing suit."

"I imagine it isn't," Brenae told her.

Caite looked at the mailboxes then back at

Brenae, and her brow crinkled. "Are you here picking up mail for someone?"

"Nope. I live here. Temporarily. Until the damn builders get off their asses and finish our house."

Caite laughed. "Thank God! For a second, I was wondering how horrible navy pay had to be for a rear admiral to be living here."

Brenae laughed with her. "We sold our other house sooner than we thought and since there weren't any open houses on the base, we just bit the bullet and put most of our stuff in storage and rented the apartment here until our house is completed."

"That makes sense. I haven't officially moved out of my apartment yet, but after everything that happened, Rocco was pretty insistent I move in here with him."

Brenae nodded. "I know we just met and all, and it's not my place to give you advice, but...moving in with someone is a big step. And I'm saying this woman to woman...be careful and don't give up your independence for a man. I mean, I like Rocco and the others on his team, but if they're anything like my husband, they like to be in charge and to get what they want."

Luckily, Caite didn't take offense. "Believe me, I know. I've thought about this long and hard. I've still got my own bank account, I'll be starting a new job soon, and honestly...I *want* to be with Rocco full time. Before everything happened, I hated sleeping in my apartment by myself. I get what you're saying though, and I appreciate it more than you know."

Brenae smiled. "It's just that I see so many young women rushing into relationships, even giving up their financial independence because they're desperate to be with a man."

"Honestly, Rocco *wants* me to work. I think he feels it'll keep me busy when he gets sent on a mission."

"He's smart. That's very true," Brenae told Caite. "After thirty years of being married to a military man, who was a SEAL for much of that time, believe me when I tell you that you *need* your own life and your own friends. More often than not, he'll miss important events in your life, although not of his own volition, and you'll need your own tribe to help you when he can't."

"Does it ever get easier?" Caite asked.

"What?"

"Missing your husband when he's gone? Worrying about him?"

"Honestly?"

Caite nodded.

"No." When the other woman's face fell, Brenae hurried to explain. "But I'd never in a million years ask Dag to do anything other than what he's doing. Even when he was gone for over six months one year, I never considered complaining to him about the time he was away from me and our kids. He was doing what he loved. Important work. And all that time away made me appreciate him more when he *was* home, and the same went for him with me. The best thing you can do for Rocco is support him. And know that even though his duty to his country is important, *you* are just as important."

"Thanks. I needed to hear that. He hasn't even been gone that much since we've been together, but I dread it."

"If you ever want to talk, I'm happy to give you my number. I know when I first started dating Dag, I had so many questions about everything."

"I appreciate it. I'd love that. I've made pretty good friends with some of the other SEAL wives, and while they're super friendly and all, I feel kinda like I'm on the outskirts when I'm with them. Not because of anything they've done, but simply because they've known each other for so long."

"You'll find your own tribe," Brenae reassured

her. "Rocco is the only one of his team to have a girl-friend, right?"

"Yeah, but how'd you know that?" Caite asked.

Brenae smiled. "I'm a rear admiral's wife. It's my job to know everything about the dependents of the men under my husband's command."

"You make me miss my mom," Caite blurted, then grimaced. "Sorry, I didn't mean that in a bad way. I'm not saying you're old or anything. Shit..." she mumbled, putting her forehead in her hand. "I'm going to shut up now before I make things worse."

"It's fine," Brenae told her with a chuckle. "You remind me of my daughter, and I miss her a lot, so we're even."

The two women smiled at each other.

Just then, they heard a commotion outside the small mailroom. Both women turned to see what was going on.

A woman was loudly berating a man at her side. Her hands gesturing wildly as she spoke.

"Holy crap," Caite breathed. "She sounds really pissed."

Brenae watched uneasily. The fight didn't sound like a normal disagreement. The woman was borderline hysterical, screaming at the man for allegedly cheating on her with the "skank in apartment 247."

The man wasn't helping matters by rolling his eyes at the woman.

Then she grabbed his arm and yanked on it. Hard.

The man jerked to a stop and turned to glare at the woman. She reached up and put both hands on his chest, shoving him. He took a step backward, then brought his hands up and pushed her right back.

Brenae gently grabbed hold of Caite's arm and pulled her back, away from the door.

"We should do something," Caite protested.

Brenae shook her head. "No."

"But what if he hurts her?"

"Do you have your phone on you?" Brenae asked, ignoring Caite's question.

She shook her head. "I left it upstairs because I was just going to grab the mail and go right back up."

Brenae's stomach clenched. She didn't have her phone either, for the same reason.

The woman's screeching stopped abruptly—and Brenae was scared to peer through the window of the mailroom to see why. Something about the situation had her hackles up from the start.

Then they heard the man let out a shocked scream, followed by a loud thud.

Caite inched forward and peered out the window.

Then she turned back to Brenae, her face white as a sheet. "She's stabbing him!"

"What?" Brenae asked in shock. She moved up beside Caite—and could hardly believe what she was seeing.

The woman was hovering over the man, who was on the ground. Her arm flew up then back down, plunging a knife into his chest even as they watched. Then she did it again. And again.

Bile rose up in Brenae's throat at what she was witnessing. The woman was out of control, plunging the knife into the man's chest, belly, and even his crotch, over and over in a completely uncontrollable frenzy.

"Step away from the window slowly," Brenae whispered to Caite.

Just then the elevator door opened nearby, and a woman walked into the lobby. She took one look at the bloody and violent murder happening right in front of her eyes and screamed at the top of her lungs.

It was enough to startle the woman with the knife. She looked up...right into Brenae's wide, shocked gaze.

Ignoring the resident who had turned and run down the hall as fast as she could, probably to the exit at the end of the hallway, the woman with the knife stood, kicked the man at her feet who was no longer moving, and headed for the mailroom with a look of malevolence on her face.

Brenae looked down and realized that the door to the mailroom didn't lock. It was a simple swinging door. She pulled on Caite's arm, yanking her backward toward the sorting table and trash bin on the opposite side of the room from the mailboxes.

"Shit, shit, shit," Caite muttered as she stumbled away from the door.

In seconds, the crazed woman kicked the door open, and it made an extremely loud bang as it slammed against the wall of the mail room.

"*You!*" she said with a malicious look in her eye as she pointed the tip of the bloody knife in her hand at Caite. "You're gonna pay for flirting with my boyfriend!"

CHAPTER FIVE

Dag ran his hand through his hair. He was tired but knew that was how he was going to feel for the next few weeks...until the navy brought in a replacement and that person was brought up to speed with operations. Dag would work himself to the bone if it meant making sure the SEALs he was ultimately responsible for were safe.

His thoughts turned to Brenae. Once again grateful that she never complained when he had to put work before her. Never got bitter when he missed important anniversaries. Never blamed him when things didn't go as they'd planned...curtesy of the US Navy. She just kept on keeping on. It was one of the million and one things he loved about her.

Lately, a hell of a lot hadn't gone as they'd

planned, the least of which was their dream house not being completed on time and them having to move into an apartment for a few months. In the scope of life, it wasn't a huge deal, but he knew how much Brenae had been looking forward to moving into the house they'd designed together.

He was lost in thought about what he could to do surprise her, when Dag's office door flew open. The door cracked against the wall behind it, and Dag was up with a knife in his hand before he'd even thought about what he was doing.

Standing there was Blake Wise...known as Rocco to his friends and teammates. "Sir! Have you heard from your wife in the last fifteen minutes?"

Shocked at the interruption and confused at the question, Dag said, "No. Why?"

"Shit! There's a hostage situation at our apartment complex. I haven't been able to get ahold of Caite. Her phone just rings before going to voicemail."

Dag immediately pulled out his cell phone and clicked on Brenae's name. He stood tensely as it began to ring, and then went to her voicemail. Usually hearing her recorded voice message soothed him, but today he impatiently waited for the beep then said, "It's me. Call the second you get this message."

"Sit-rep," he barked at Rocco as he walked toward him, grabbing his keys on the way.

Turning, Rocco headed out of the office and the two men strode down the hall toward the stairwell, side by side at a fast clip.

"One of my neighbors called and told me that SWAT and San Diego PD were headed for the apartment complex. They were being told to shelter in place inside their apartments and not to let anyone inside until the cops showed up. He was watching out his window and saw the unit being surrounded. I called a contact I know in the PD and he said there was a report of a hostage situation near the lobby."

Dag's heart almost stopped beating. He had no reason to think his Brenae was involved, but the hair on the back of his neck was standing straight up, a sure sign something wasn't right.

Without another word, the two men burst out of the building on the naval base and jogged toward Dag's Land Rover. At that moment, they weren't superior officer and subordinate, they were two men desperate to make sure their women were safe.

On the way to the apartment complex, Rocco tried once more to get ahold of Caite, with no luck.

Dag wasn't able to get near the parking lot for the complex because of the police presence, so he simply left his SUV parked along a side street.

It wasn't often that Dag pulled rank, but he didn't give a shit if someone accused him of using the fact he was one of the highest-ranking men on the naval base to get his way. He'd do whatever it took to get to Brenae.

He walked up to a police captain and said, "I'm Rear Admiral Dag Creasy and many of my sailors live in this building. I need a sit-rep, and I need it *now*."

The captain looked surprised, but immediately told him what he knew. "We got a call about forty minutes ago from a hysterical woman who said she'd just witnessed a murder. When we got here, a hostage situation was in progress. We locked the building down and have all the exits covered. We're waiting for more personnel to arrive and then we'll try to establish contact with the perpetrator."

Dag looked toward the entrance to the apartment complex—and his legs almost buckled when he saw the outline of a body lying near the front doors. "Who's the victim?" he asked.

"We aren't sure. Looks to be a male in his mid-twenties though."

Ashamed at the relief that coursed through his body—the man was someone's brother, son, or father—Dag nodded. He looked over at Rocco and saw the SEAL's entire concentration was directed on the front doors.

"Do you know who the hostages are yet?" Dag asked.

"Not their names, but there's two of them. Women. One older, one younger. The perp is a woman in her mid-twenties, and initial information states that she's most likely on something."

"Sir—" Rocco said urgently next to him.

Dag held up his hand, stopping the SEAL from saying anything. He needed as much information as he could get from the police captain before deciding on his next move. "Where are they?"

"Apparently inside the mailroom just off the lobby."

Dag's mind spun. He had no doubt now that his Brenae was inside that room. She always went down to check the mail around the same time every morning. She was a creature of habit, no matter how many times he'd warned her to change up her schedule for safety's sake.

"Here's the deal," he told the captain. "I'm eighty-five percent sure one of the hostages is my wife. I know this is your scene and your responsibility, but with all due respect, that's my woman in there."

"And mine," Rocco said in a low, deadly tone.

"We need in on this op," Dag said. "I've got fifteen years of SEAL experience under my belt and Rocco here is currently a SEAL himself. Let us help you. Too much time has passed as it is. Use our expertise to end this sooner rather than later."

The captain eyed Dag critically for a long moment. "How good are you at negotiations?"

"I'm the best," Dag said. And he wasn't bragging.

"Go see the sergeant over there and put on vests before you go near that building," the captain said. When Dag and Rocco turned to head toward where he'd pointed, the captain said, "This isn't Iraq. The American public doesn't like hearing about public executions."

Dag nodded. He got it. The police were fighting an uphill battle in the court of public opinion and the last thing the city of Riverton—or the US Navy, for that matter—needed was to kill a young woman, even if she was a murderer and threatening the person he loved most in this world.

Within minutes, Dag and Rocco had donned black bulletproof vests with the words SWAT on the back over their naval battle dress uniform.

Dag was very aware of the knife in the sheath at the small of his back, and assumed Rocco was similarly armed. They had no guns, but didn't need any. Their skills as SEALs would be a hell of a lot more effective. Besides, shooting a weapon inside the small mailroom meant possibly hitting Brenae or Caite.

"How we going to play this?" Rocco asked as they strode toward the doors of the lobby.

"Any fucking way we have to," Dag told him grimly.

Brenae stared at the woman pacing back and forth in front of her. It was obvious the woman was under the influence of something, and she didn't think it was alcohol. Her movements were erratic and she hadn't stopped mumbling to herself since her original threat toward Caite.

Luckily, something in the lobby had distracted her before she'd tried to do anything about the alleged flirting she'd thought Caite had done with her now-deceased boyfriend, then it was as if she'd forgotten all about them. She'd started mumbling under her breath and pacing, seemingly oblivious to her boyfriend lying dead on the floor near the lobby doors.

Brenae had forced Caite into the corner of the small room then positioned herself in front of the younger woman. She'd put her finger to her lips, indicating that Caite shouldn't say a word and after she nodded, they both waited tensely to see what would happen next.

Wishing she had her phone to let Dag know what was happening, Brenae didn't take her eyes from the distraught woman pacing back and forth. They'd all heard the sirens and knew the building was most likely surrounded. Brenae was thankful now that the door to the small room didn't lock. It would make it easier for the police to get inside.

Brenae had the thought that maybe she should try to get to know their captor. Learn her name. Find out what the fight with her dead boyfriend was about. But the longer the standoff went on, the crazier the woman acted. Hitting herself in the head now and then, running the bloody knife over her forearm, and looking up at the ceiling as if something was written there. Brenae figured it was better to wait silently and hope the woman forgot they were there at all.

A motion at the door caught her attention, and

Brenae sucked in a breath when she saw Dag standing there. He had on a black vest that she'd never seen before and was holding his hands up, letting the woman pacing know he wasn't armed.

"Get back!" the woman screamed, pointing the knife at the door.

"We just want to talk," Dag said.

"No! No talking!" She didn't even let him say another word. She spun and reached over and grabbed Brenae's arm, hauling her up in front of her. In seconds, the bloody knife was at her throat.

Brenae managed not to scream as she kept her eyes locked on her husband's. The tip of the knife pressed into her skin, and she did her best not to think about communicable diseases or the fact that she could die, feet from her husband.

"Let her go." Dag's voice was no longer cajoling and easy. He'd gone from trying to be nice to a deadly Navy SEAL in a heartbeat.

Brenae saw Rocco standing behind her husband, the same focused, lethal look on his face.

Crazily, seeing them there, knowing they'd do whatever it took to make sure she got out of this alive, made her relax. Dag had never let her down. This is what he did. What he'd spent his life doing.

She never thought she'd be a damsel in distress, but here she was.

"Put the knife down," she said softly and gently.

"I can't!" the woman moaned.

"Yes, you can," Brenae coaxed.

The knife pricked her a bit harder, and Brenae felt a trickle of blood ooze from the nick and trail downward, stopped by the collar of the T-shirt she was wearing.

Swallowing hard, she looked into Dag's eyes once more. He didn't blink, just met her gaze steadily.

Why wasn't he giving her some sort of signal? He should be telling her what to do telepathically.

She mentally rolled her eyes. It wasn't as if he *could* talk to her telepathically. She had to get her shit together. Did Dag want her to throw herself to the right? To the left? When? Before he did something? After? They hadn't ever talked about this. About what to do if she was in a hostage situation and Dag had to rescue her.

Brenae knew she was on the verge of freaking out, but she had no idea what to do.

"They need to leave! Why won't they leave?" the woman grumbled behind her.

Then, with a clarity Brenae didn't have a second ago, she knew what she had to do.

The knife was probably going to dig into her skin when she moved, but then again, the woman might decide to just kill her anyway. Then she'd go after Caite. Brenae wasn't a SEAL, or a soldier, or anything of the sort, but there was no way she was going to let the younger woman be put into *another* situation like she'd been in a week ago. She'd been through enough.

Brenae met her husband's eyes once more—but this time, she quickly glanced to her right. Then she did it again.

When Dag's chin dipped in acknowledgement, she relaxed.

He'd take care of this. Of *her*.

"I need to get out of here!" the woman wailed. "Why'd he have to dis me like that? It's *his* fault. And yours! *You* made him cheat!"

The woman was obviously delusional if she thought the young man lying in a puddle of blood on the other side of the door had *ever* flirted with Brenae. She was at least twice his age.

Knowing it was now or never, Brenae took a deep breath, looked at Dag one final time—then threw herself as hard as she could to the right.

CHAPTER SIX

Dag held back his fury by the skin of his teeth. He'd never been in a situation like this. Never had to stand by helplessly as his wife was in imminent danger. He now knew exactly how Rocco had felt when his woman had been in the hands of a madman the other week.

He wanted to tell Brenae not to worry, that he'd get her out of this...but he couldn't. Not with the obviously out-of-her-mind woman holding that knife to Brenae's throat.

Then he saw his brave-as-fuck wife look to her right. Then she did it again.

He wanted to shake his head. To tell her not to do it. But honestly, he saw no other way out of this situation. He had to get inside the mailroom, and in the time it would take him, the drugged-out woman could shove the knife deeply into Brenae's throat.

She needed to do what Caite had done the week before. Take herself out of the equation and let him do what he did best.

Tensing his muscles, he heard Rocco whisper from behind him, "Steady, Sir..."

He moved just as he saw Brenae's muscles bunch in preparation.

The door flew open from his weight as his wife threw herself to the side.

Before she'd even hit the floor, the knife that had been at her throat was thrown across the room and the woman who'd dared take his wife hostage was face-down on the floor with his knee in her back.

The woman fought like she was possessed. It took all of Dag's and Rocco's combined strength to subdue her, and even then she refused to give up. It wasn't until five more members of the San Diego SWAT team entered the small room and hogtied her that she finally sagged in surrender. One second she was fighting like a wildcat, and the next she was practically comatose.

Not sparing a second thought for the deranged and drugged-out woman, Dag turned to where Brenae had thrown herself. She was crouched against the wall, her arms around Caite, comforting her.

His woman had just had a knife to her throat and *she* was comforting Caite.

Feeling as if he were a hundred years old, Dag shuffled over to where she was sitting. Rocco got there at the same time and pulled Caite to her feet and into his arms. Dag didn't think he could even stand. His eyes locked on the blood staining Brenae's collar. The mark on her neck was still bleeding and for a second, he couldn't even think.

The red on her skin was obscene in a way he couldn't even describe. He'd seen a lot of blood and death in his lifetime, but never in this context. Never on his Brenae.

"Good Lord, Caite! I moved you into my apartment because I thought you'd be safer," Dag heard Rocco saying as he carried her out of the room.

As if she knew exactly how off-kilter Dag was at the moment, Brenae opened her arms.

One second he was staring at the blood on her neck, and the next he was burying his nose in her hair. She smelled like she always did, like flowers. She hardly ever used the same scented lotion two days in a row, but she always smelled fresh and clean. Today was no exception.

"I'm okay," she said softly into his ear as her arms closed around him.

Dag's breath hitched in his throat and he squeezed his eyes closed. He'd almost lost her.

That had been too close. *Way* too close.

He couldn't speak, simply tightened his hold on her.

"I'm okay," she repeated. Then said it again. And again.

Nothing else mattered in that moment. Not the police officers carrying the drugged-out woman out of the room. Not the captain entering the room and ordering the remaining officers to be careful of the knife.

Brenae moved and took his face in her hands. He opened his eyes to look into her beautiful blue gaze. "You got here in time," she told him softly.

His eyes dropped to her neck once more...and just like that, the odd lethargy that had taken hold of him disappeared like a puff of smoke. He turned his head to look at the police captain. "My wife needs medical attention."

"Dag, no, I'm okay."

"Now," Dag ordered the captain, ignoring his wife. He knew he was being a dick, but he'd be damned if Brenae waited a second longer than she already had to have someone look at her injury.

Deciding Rocco had the right idea and the paramedics were taking too long, Dag got to his feet, leaned over and picked Brenae up. He might be half a century old, but he hoped he never got too old to carry his wife around.

She looped her arms around his neck and relaxed into him.

Thankful she wasn't fighting him, Dag walked out of the mailroom, through the lobby, past the young man's dead body on the floor and out into the bright sunlight. It was weird; it felt like hours had gone by since the time he'd learned about the situation at the apartment complex, but in reality, less than an hour had passed.

He walked up to one of the ambulances parked in the lot and simply climbed inside with the woman who meant more to him than anything in the world. As he placed her down on the gurney, Brenae looked up at him and smiled. "My Hero."

Thirty minutes later, after telling the police captain that he was absolutely *not* going to come to the station to give his statement until the next day because he needed to see to his wife, and after the paramedics cleaned up Brenae's neck and put a small bandage over the superficial cut, Dag opened their apartment door and followed his wife inside.

His plan was to get her into her pajamas, put her on the couch under one of her favorite fluffy blankets, and make her a huge bowl of chicken noodle soup. But it seemed Brenae had different ideas.

The second the door closed behind them, she pushed him backward until his back hit the door and went to her knees. Her fingers frantically worked at the belt around his waist.

Dag covered her fingers with his own. "Hon—" he started, but she violently shook her head.

"No. I *need* this. I need *you*"

She got the belt undone and within seconds, his zipper was down and his cock was in her hand. Brenae licked her lips and pumped his shaft with her hand a few times, before engulfing him in her mouth.

It had been a long time since Dag had seen his wife this desperate. But the longer he watched her pleasure him, the more her desperation transferred itself to him.

He could've lost her today.

She could've had her throat slit right in front of him.

She could've fucking *died*.

Growling, Dag reached down and grabbed Brenae under the arms and hauled her off his dick. He picked her up around the waist and shuffled toward their bedroom. His pants were around his ankles, but he didn't give a shit.

Brenae attacked his mouth as if she were a dying woman and his lips held the cure to her survival. Their teeth clashed together as their heads tilted back and forth, trying to get deeper inside one another.

Feeling a primal need to fuck, to prove to himself, and her, that they were both alive and well, Dag dropped his arms when he felt the backs of her knees hit the edge of their bed. "Take your pants off," he ordered, even as he reached for the drawer of their nightstand. He pulled out the small bottle of lube they kept there and waited impatiently for Brenae to get naked. The second she was, he turned her until she was bent over the mattress.

She whimpered, but he knew it was an impatient sound, not one of distress. He didn't have time to get her wet and ready for him the way he usually did. He'd worship her slowly in a while. For now, he needed to be inside her more than he'd needed anything in his life.

He squirted a generous amount of lube onto his cock and grunted in pleasure when he wrapped his hand around himself to spread it around.

"Hurry, Dag," Brenae begged from her bent position.

Looking down, he saw her fingers frantically playing with her clit. Smiling, he covered his fingers with more lube and pushed her hand out of the way. Without hesitation, he thrust his slippery fingers inside her body, and she moaned, arching her back, giving him better access to where he most wanted to be.

A minute later, when he was satisfied he'd lubricated her enough so she could take him without pain, Dag lined his weeping cock up with her slit and entered her with one hard thrust.

He held himself still inside her, enjoying the connection and the feeling of her twitching around his dick.

He almost lost this. Would've never felt her warm, wet body surround his again. Never heard her laughter. Never seen her smile. The thoughts were almost enough to make him lose his erection altogether.

"Dag, stop thinking so damn hard and fuck me already!" Brenae complained impatiently.

He smiled. Leave it to his wife to pull him out of his own head. "You can't ever leave me," he said as he pulled out and slammed back inside her. "Ever. Never. Hear me?" He punctuated each word with a flex of his hips, fucking her even as he scolded her for something he knew she had no control over.

"I won't," she agreed. Her fingers flexed against the comforter under her and she stood on her tiptoes, trying to get closer to him as he fucked her.

"I love you so much, Brenae. You're my life. My reason for living. I can't handle a world without you in it." His words were gentle and tender, but his love-making was anything but. He held her hips still and slammed into her over and over again, showing her how much he loved fucking her. Making love to her.

"I love you too," she gasped. "Yes, God, Dag, *yes*. More. Harder!"

He loved when she got so turned on she couldn't even speak in full sentences. Deciding they'd done enough talking, Dag concentrated on making sure he pleasured his wife. Bending over her, his hips continuing their frenzied movement, he shoved a hand under her body. His fingers found his target and flicked against her clit, hard and fast, showing her no mercy.

Brenae jerked in his grip and her head flew backward as she arched and pushed back against him.

Loving how passionate his wife was, Dag continued his assault on her senses.

Within a minute, he knew she was close to coming...which was a good thing, because his balls had drawn up in preparation for their own release. Loving the continuous moans that left her mouth and the way she shuddered under him, Dag grunted in satisfaction when he felt the tell-tale ripples of her inner muscles against his cock.

"That's it. Come for me."

With a loud moan, she did.

Dag had the momentary thought that he wanted to pull out and see his come shoot all over her ass, but knew it was too late for that. The come burst from the tip of his cock as if he were a boy experiencing his first lay. His dick throbbed in time with his heartbeat as he pumped his essence into Brenae.

He came so long and hard, he felt his release seeping out of her pussy, but when it came to sex, nothing fazed either of them anymore. When he felt as if he could move without his knees giving out,

Dag slowly pulled out of her. They both groaned in disappointment.

Then Brenae braced herself up on her hands and turned around to look at him. She smiled and licked her lips. Dag's dick twitched, but it would be a while before he got hard enough to fuck her again.

"Climb up," he ordered, gesturing to the bed with his head.

Brenae immediately moved, tearing her shirt up and off her body as she did. Her bra followed. Dag stripped off his clothes, thanking God he hadn't tripped over his pants in his haste to get them both to their bedroom.

He got on the bed with Brenae and took her into his arms. They lay there for a long moment, enjoying the cuddle time after the intense love-making they'd just experienced. It had been months since they'd gone after each other like that. Shit, he hadn't even taken off his clothes. Dag's arms tightened. "I love you."

"And I love you," she purred.

"I wanted to coddle you," Dag said.

"I don't need coddling," she told him. "Haven't you figured that out yet?"

He chuckled, then sobered. He kissed her temple. "I'm gonna call those builders and light a fire under their asses. I need you in our house. With our alarm system. Safe."

"I'm always safe when I'm with you," she said.

Dag pressed his lips together tightly to try to keep his composure. Brenae always knew the exact right thing to say. "How's your neck?"

"It's fine."

"No pain?"

"No."

"As much as I like you taking control and attacking me in the foyer of our place, I'm still feeling the need to coddle you," he informed her.

"Yeah?"

"Yup."

She smirked up at him. "Well, then, coddle away, sailor."

And he did.

CHAPTER SEVEN

Today was the day.

After Brenae had been held hostage in the mailroom of the apartment complex, Dag was done being patient with the contractor. He'd called and threatened and browbeat the poor man until he'd done as he'd originally promised and finished their house on time.

Dag had kept the details from Brenae, not wanting to get her hopes up and then have them dashed if the house was once more was delayed.

Smiling, Dag picked up his cell and clicked on his wife's name. She answered after only one ring.

"Hi, hon. What's up?"

"Where are you?"

"At the apartment. Why? What's wrong?"

"Nothing's wrong. I have a surprise for you. I'll be there to pick you up in about fifteen minutes."

"What on earth? Dag, it's the middle of the day. I thought you had that meeting this afternoon?"

"I did, but I postponed it. This is more important."

"You're worrying me," Brenae said.

"Don't be worried," Dag told his wife. "Just get dressed and be ready to go in fifteen minutes when I get there."

After a few more minutes of small talk, Brenae agreed. They said their goodbyes and Dag smiled all the way to the apartment complex. They'd have a lot of work ahead of them in the next few days, but he'd done what he could to mitigate that, hiring a company to move their boxes from storage into their new house. He'd snuck out of work a couple days that week to set up the surprise waiting for his wife at the house, but they still had to move the stuff from the apartment and, of course, unpack.

Jogging up the three flights of stairs to the third floor, Dag unlocked their apartment door and wasn't surprised to see Brenae ready and waiting for him. Refusing to answer her million-and-one questions, he reveled in her bafflement when he held out a blindfold once they were seated inside his car.

"Really?" she asked with an eyebrow arched.

"Really," he confirmed.

Showing that she was a good sport, Brenae tied the cloth around her head and muttered, "This better be good."

Dag leaned over and gently took her chin in his hand and turned her head. He kissed her until they were both breathing hard. "It'll be worth it," he whispered, then leaned forward and kissed her forehead before sitting back in his seat and starting the car.

They held hands the entire way to their new house. If Brenae had an inkling of where he was taking her, she didn't say anything. It took about thirty minutes to get there, but when he pulled into their driveway, the view of the ocean took his breath away, as always.

The house they'd built wasn't huge...it didn't need to be for just the two of them. There were two extra rooms for when the grandkids came to visit, as well as a giant master bedroom and gourmet kitchen. But it was the deck that Dag had brought his wife to see.

"Wait here. I'll come around and get you," he told her.

Brenae nodded and sat with her hands in her lap patiently.

He opened the car door and reached down, taking her hand in his. Brenae didn't hesitate, she trusted him one hundred percent, and that blind trust never failed to humble Dag. He wrapped his arm around her waist and held her to his side as he steered her around the house to the back. There wasn't much yard to speak of, but the huge deck more than made up for the lack of foliage. He helped her climb the stairs of the deck to get to the top, loving the small smile on Brenae's face.

Glancing at the hot tub, Dag vowed to take advantage of the privacy the house and yard provided to fuck his wife as she stood in the bubbling water, staring out at the vista in front of them.

He guided Brenae to the exact spot he'd scoped out earlier and turned her so her back was to his chest. He leaned down and whispered, "Ready?"

"Ready," she answered immediately.

Dag reached up and gently untied the knot on the piece of cloth and let it fall to the wooden slats at their feet.

Her startled gasp was the reaction he'd hoped for.

"Oh, Dag. It's beautiful!"

And it was. The sun reflecting off the Pacific

Ocean was absolutely stunning. There was a breeze coming off the water and the sand was pristine. There wasn't one person on the private beach at the end of the wooden walkway from their property. It was serene. Calm. And all theirs.

Brenae turned and threw her arms around Dag's neck. "I know we've seen this view more times than I can count, but somehow, standing here without the construction chaos around us, and on our finished deck...the view is even better than I dreamed it would be. Can we go inside?"

"Yeah, Brenae. Of course we can go inside. It's our house."

She blinked. "But it's not done yet. I thought we agreed not to tour it again until it was completed."

"It *is* done," Dag said with a small grin.

"Seriously?"

"Seriously."

She grinned. "You must've thrown some of that naval rank around in order to achieve that, huh, sailor?"

He returned the smile. "After seeing you with a knife to your throat, nothing was going to keep me from making sure this house was completed sooner rather than later."

"I love you," Brenae told him.

"And I love you. Come on. I have something else to show you."

"Something else?" she asked with a smirk, moving her hand to palm one of his ass cheeks and squeeze. "Is it in here?"

Dag laughed, but simply took her hand in his and headed for the door. He walked her through the kitchen, the dining room, the living area, smiling as she oohed and ahhed over all the work that had been done since the last time she'd seen the shell of the house. Ignoring the boxes of their stuff, he walked down the hall to their master bedroom.

The door was shut, and he paused dramatically in front of it—before throwing open the door.

There were no boxes of belongings to be unpacked here. He'd made sure their four-poster bed was set up, and that there were clean linens on it. The curtains had been thrown back, spilling the afternoon light over everything. Their dresser was there, full of clothes, as was the bookshelf with all the signed romances she'd collected over the years.

The room was ready to be slept in. They might have a lot more work in their future, but here, in their space, they could relax.

"Oh my God, Dag! It's perfect," Brenae said.

"I love you, Brenae. How in the hell you've put up

with me over the years, I'll never understand. I wish I could give you the world, but you'll have to settle for this one little piece of it."

Brenae didn't respond with words, she simply stood up on tiptoe and kissed him. Long and hard. Dag backed them up until his knees hit the mattress. He gripped her waist and pulled her down on top of him as he fell. She giggled, and they both adjusted until they were lying cross-wise on the bed. Brenae's hair falling around her shoulders and tickling his face.

"I wanted our room to be completely done so you'd have a place to go that wasn't full of boxes and stuff."

"I love it."

Dag lifted his head and kissed her hard. Then he put his arms over his head and said with a smirk, "So, now that you've got me here, what are you going to do with me?"

Brenae smiled and immediately reached for the buttons of his uniform. As she quickly undid them, she said, "I think I'm gonna ravish you, soldier."

"Sounds good to me," he told her.

The next minute was consumed with both of them trying to get their clothes off while not losing contact with one another. Finally, when they were both naked, Dag grabbed Brenae by the hips and tugged her up so she was straddling his face.

"I thought I," she gasped as he ran his tongue from her slit to her clit, "was supposed to ravish *you*."

Dag paused in his attention to his wife's pussy long enough to say, "You can ravish me after."

"Um...okay," Brenae got out before gasping once more as Dag got to work eating out his wife.

Ten minutes later, his face was soaked with her juices and she'd almost smothered him when she'd come, but he couldn't stop grinning.

When Brenae caught her breath, she scooted back down his body, with Dag's help, and settled herself over his cock, which was as hard as steel.

Without a word, she lifted, grabbed hold of him, and notched his weeping cock head to her slit. Dag wanted to lift his hips and thrust inside her hard and fast, but he held himself still, wanting to make sure he didn't do anything that would hurt her.

When he felt their pubic hair mesh together, he looked down in satisfaction. "Fuck, that is so sexy," he murmured.

Then she moved, and his cock glistened with her excitement.

"And that's even more so," he said in appreciation.

Brenae started moving on him in earnest. Her thighs strained with the effort it took to undulate on his lap and her tits bounced up and down with her movements. Dag couldn't keep the smile from his face. She was his. All fucking his.

He loved watching her get off on him. One hand went to her clit, and she began to play with herself as she bobbed up and down. The other hand rested on his chest, propping herself up. When she began to slow down, Dag brought his hands to her hips and helped lift her up and down on his cock.

He felt her legs begin to shake with her second impending orgasm and he was silently grateful. He'd been on the verge of coming since the moment she'd eased herself down on him.

The second her vaginal muscles clamped down on his dick as she began to come, he lost it as well. Hauling her down on him and holding her as tightly as he could, burying himself inside her as far as possible, Dag exploded, but didn't take his eyes from his wife.

Her nipples were hard and her chest was flushed red. Her hips continued to undulate as she tried to make her orgasm last as long as possible. Her fingernails dug into his chest, and he'd never seen anything more beautiful in his entire life. The afternoon sun shone on them, their sweat glistening in the light.

After a minute or so, Brenae finally came down from the orgasmic high and Dag caught her as she collapsed on his chest. Her warm breath feathered over his neck and goose bumps broke out on his arms. He felt his dick gradually soften, and after a bit, he popped out from inside her. The rush of their mixed come dripped down his shaft onto his balls, soaking the sheet under them.

He chuckled.

"What's funny?" she murmured.

"We're a mess," he said.

"Yup. Which isn't surprising," she said.

"We should clean up."

At that, Brenae lifted her head. "Seriously? You want to move? Now?"

"We've got a hot tub ready and waiting for us," Dag said, waggling his eyebrows suggestively.

Brenae giggled. Then she sobered and rested her forehead on his. "Thank you."

"For what?"

"For everything. This house. Our kids. Our life. Things haven't always been smooth sailing, but not once have I ever doubted your love for me."

"Good," Dag said. "Because when push comes to

shove, you are the most important thing in my life. I'd move heaven and earth to see your smile. To hear you laugh. If you asked me to build you a hundred houses, I'd do it just to make you happy."

Brenae smiled. "I think this one is perfect. I don't need a hundred."

Dag brought his hands up and pushed her hair out of her face. Then he kissed her, a sweet closed-mouth kiss, before saying, "You made me a better man. Every day I wonder what you'd think of my actions, and it grounds me."

Tears filled Brenae's eyes, but she didn't speak.

"I love you, hon. You'll never know how much."

"I do know how much, because I love you exactly the same way."

He smiled up at her. "So...wanna try out the hot tub?"

She huffed a laugh. "Yes."

In a heartbeat, Dag had slid out from under Brenae and lifted her in his arms. She squealed and threw her arms around his neck.

"I should've carried you across the threshold, but since I figure we'll be spending quite a bit of time naked in our hot tub, I might as well carry you into *that* for the first time instead. Yeah?"

"Sounds perfect to me."

Later that night, as Brenae slept in his arms, Dag thought back over their life together. He'd been serious earlier when he'd told his wife that he didn't know what he ever did to deserve her. She was the best thing that ever happened to him, and he vowed to do whatever it took to make her happy for the rest of her life.

He fell asleep with a smile on his face, secure in the knowledge that Brenae was safe in his arms.

*

For more of the SEAL of Protection: Legacy series, check out the next book in the series, *Securing Sidney*

ABOUT THE AUTHOR

New York Times, *USA Today* and *Wall Street Journal* Bestselling Author Susan Stoker has a heart as big as the state of Tennessee where she lives, but this all American girl has also spent the last fourteen years living in Missouri, California, Colorado, Indiana, and Texas. She's married to a retired Army man who now gets to follow *her* around the country.

She debuted her first series in 2014 and quickly followed that up with the SEAL of Protection Series, which solidified her love of writing and creating stories readers can get lost in.

If you enjoyed this book, or any book, please consider leaving a review. It's appreciated by authors more than you'll know.

www.stokeraces.com
www.AcesPress.com
susan@stokeraces.com

facebook.com/authorsusanstoker

twitter.com/Susan_Stoker

instagram.com/authorsusanstoker

goodreads.com/SusanStoker

bookbub.com/authors/susan-stoker

amazon.com/author/susanstoker

Also by Susan Stoker

Delta Force Heroes Series

Rescuing Rayne

Rescuing Aimee (novella)

Rescuing Emily

Rescuing Harley

Marrying Emily (novella)

Rescuing Kassie

Rescuing Bryn

Rescuing Casey

Rescuing Sadie (novella)

Rescuing Wendy

Rescuing Mary

Rescuing Macie (novella)

Badge of Honor: Texas Heroes Series

Justice for Mackenzie

Justice for Mickie

Justice for Corrie

Justice for Laine (novella)

Shelter for Elizabeth

Justice for Boone

Shelter for Adeline

Shelter for Sophie

Justice for Erin

Justice for Milena

Shelter for Blythe

Justice for Hope

Shelter for Quinn

Shelter for Koren (June 2019)

Shelter for Penelope (Oct 2019)

SEAL of Protection: Legacy Series

Securing Caite

Securing Brenae (novella)

Securing Sidney (May 2019)

Securing Piper (Sept 2019)

Securing Zoey (Jan 2020)

Securing Avery (TBA)

Securing Kalee (TBA)

Ace Security Series

Claiming Grace

Claiming Alexis

Claiming Bailey

Claiming Felicity

Claiming Sarah (Sept 2019)

Mountain Mercenaries Series

Defending Allye

Defending Chloe
Defending Morgan
Defending Harlow (July 2019)
Defending Everly (Dec 2019)
Defending Zara (TBA)
Defending Raven (TBA)

SEAL of Protection Series

Protecting Caroline
Protecting Alabama
Protecting Fiona
Marrying Caroline (novella)
Protecting Summer
Protecting Cheyenne
Protecting Jessyka
Protecting Julie (novella)
Protecting Melody
Protecting the Future
Protecting Kiera (novella)
Protecting Alabama's Kids (novella)
Protecting Dakota

Stand Alone

The Guardian Mist
Nature's Rift
A Princess for Cale

A Moment in Time- A Collection of Short Stories
Lambert's Lady

Special Operations Fan Fiction

http://www.AcesPress.com

Beyond Reality Series

Outback Hearts
Flaming Hearts
Frozen Hearts

Writing as Annie George:

Stepbrother Virgin (erotic novella)

SECURING SIDNEY SAMPLE

For Sidney Hale, rescuing dogs is more than a hobby. It's a calling. A deep-seated need. An unstoppable compulsion. For reasons so unsettling, she shares them with no one...until she meets Decker. After coming to her rescue while Sidney battled to save a dog—literally—the gorgeous SEAL proves he can be trusted with her secrets, her safety...maybe even her heart.

Saving an abused pit bull from a suspected dog fighter brings Decker "Gumby" Kincade not only the dog he's always wanted, but the first woman in ages to catch his interest. Sidney's reason for rescuing Hannah, and animals like her, is shocking...but it makes Gumby want her even more. Her harrowing past has made her the strong, brave, compassionate woman she is today. She could be The One...if Gumby can help curb her habit of putting herself squarely in danger's path.

But he may be too late. Hannah's previous owner is enraged over her loss...and looking for revenge.

CHAPTER ONE

Decker "Gumby" Kincade pulled into the veterinarian's office and couldn't help but smile as the woman who'd been following him as closely as she'd dared pulled in next to him. Her beat-up old Honda Accord had seen better days, but she didn't seem to notice or care that it was making a weird clanking noise.

By the time he had his truck door open, she was there.

"How'd she do? Is she okay? Was she crying?" The woman barked the questions at him, not giving Gumby time to answer the first before asking the second.

Sidney Hale was quite the contradiction. Her long black hair was in disarray from the fist fight he'd interrupted. She had a black eye forming, which just seemed to bring out the blue in her eyes even more. Her lip was swollen and still bleeding a little. The T-shirt she wore was torn and she had dirt on her jeans and hands.

But she obviously didn't care one whit about her own health; she had eyes only for the pathetic and hurt dog on the passenger-side seat of his truck.

Gumby shut the door and walked around the truck, Sidney right on his heels. "She did fine. Didn't hear a peep from her the entire way."

"Man, that's amazing. She's got to be hurting!" Sidney exclaimed. "I can't believe that asshole abused her like that. Are you sure this is a good vet? Maybe we should take her to the one I usually use."

Gumby ignored her as he opened the door and leaned in to gently pick up the bleeding and abused dog he'd named Hannah. Once again, the pit bull didn't try to bite him or otherwise show any aggression whatsoever. She *was* shaking though. "Easy, girl," Gumby murmured as he used his hip to shut the door of the truck.

As he walked toward the door, he looked at Sidney. "The vets here are great. Relax, Sidney."

She looked like she wanted to say something, but because they were at the doors, she rushed ahead to open them for him. He opened his mouth to tell the receptionist that he had an emergency, but Sidney beat him to it.

"We've got an injured dog here. We need to see a doctor immediately!"

The receptionist stood and gestured for them to follow her. Gumby was surprised when he felt Sidney's hand land on the small of his back, and she practically glued herself to his side as they entered the small treatment room.

"A technician will be here momentarily to get your information and triage your pet."

"Oh but she's—"

"Thank you," Gumby said, interrupting Sidney.

When the lady had left, Sidney turned to him and frowned. "Why'd you cut me off?"

"The last thing I want is for them to think Hannah is a stray or unwanted, because she's not."

Sidney opened her mouth to say something, but a technician burst into the room before she could say a word.

"I heard we have an emergency. What's— Oh my!"

Gumby very gently placed Hannah on the raised table in the room and kept his hand on her head. "Yeah. It's bad."

"What happened?" the vet tech breathed.

"She was taken out of my yard," Gumby lied. "And we think the guy who took her was training her to be a bait dog or something for illegal dog fighting. He poured something caustic on her back, and it looks like she was dragged behind a car. Maybe he was trying to train her and get her to run, but she couldn't keep up."

"Poor baby," The tech crooned, leaning over to pet Hannah.

The hackles on the back of the dog's neck rose and she growled low in her throat.

"Hannah," Gumby said in a low, hard tone. The dog immediately stopped and whimpered instead. "Sorry about that," he told the technician. "She's usually very docile, but we don't know what was done to her between when she was taken and when we got her back just now."

"Of course," the woman said. "It'll take her some time to trust again." She handed over a couple sheets of paper to Sidney. "I'll need you to fill those out and the doctor should be in here in a few minutes." She turned to Hannah. "Hang on, girl. We'll have you fixed up in a jiffy."

The second the woman left the room, Sidney turned to Gumby and whisper-yelled, "Why'd you tell them she was stolen out of your yard? That was stupid."

Gumby ran his hand over Hannah's head and didn't miss the way the dog sighed in contentment and tried to crawl closer to him.

"What should I have said? That I just met the dog thirty minutes ago when you were in a fistfight with the asshole who had abused her? That you stole her from him? You think that would've gotten her treated any faster?" He went on before she could answer his rhetorical questions. "No. They would've wanted to know more details, and when we admitted that we know nothing about Hannah's history, they might've been reluctant to treat her. This way she'll get the medical care she needs as soon as possible. Besides, I'm keeping her."

Gumby had been thinking about getting a dog for a while now. Ever since he'd almost died in Bahrain on his last mission. He'd always regretted not having one, and Hannah seemed to have been dropped in his lap. It was a sign—and Gumby was a big believer in them.

"We should go through the coordinator at the local rescue group I work with. I was going to bring her there. They get medical attention for the dogs that need it, and they do extensive background checks on potential adopters," Sidney told him.

"You do this a lot?" he asked.

"Do what?"

"Track down people you think are up to no good on social media? Then spy on them and, when they cross the line, take on men twice your size in order to rescue the animals they're abusing?"

Without blinking, Sidney said, "Yes."

It was Gumby's turn to be surprised. "Seriously?"

She nodded. "The animals are innocent. They didn't ask to be throw into a pit to fight another dog. Or to be starved. Or to be chained up in a backyard for their entire lives. I'll take on whoever I have to in order to save a helpless, innocent animal."

"You ever gotten in trouble because of it?"

She grinned. "You mean do the low-life bastards who are being abusive assholes turn me in? No. They've all been too busy trying to protect themselves and stay under the radar of the cops to file complaints against me."

Gumby thought she looked a little too pleased with herself. But there was something in her eyes as she explained how she championed animals—guilt. And now he wanted to know why. Wanted to know her story.

His attention was diverted when the veterinarian entered the room. She was all business, and the next ten minutes was taken up with her examining poor Hannah and getting as much information as she could from Gumby...which wasn't much. He told her to do a full blood panel on Hannah as he wasn't sure what had been done to her since she'd been taken. He wasn't proud of his lies, but if they helped get Hannah the care she needed and deserved, so be it.

The vet agreed that it looked like some sort of acid had been poured onto her back and that she'd been dragged. The dog had no toenails left and the pads of her feet had been worn off. It was the vet's opinion that her back looked worse than it probably was. She didn't think the hair would grow back, but she thought the wound should heal up pretty well.

When they went to take Hannah to the back to treat her, however, the mild-mannered dog disappeared and she began growling at the vet and her assistant.

Taken aback, the vet said, "Maybe you should come back with us. Just until we manage to get her sedated."

"Sedated?" Gumby asked.

"Yeah. Cleaning these wounds is gonna hurt, and I'd rather not harm her any more than I have to."

Gumby immediately nodded. "Right. Okay, we can come with you."

"I think just you," the vet said, giving her assistant a look Gumby couldn't interpret. "Your... friend can stay and fill out the paperwork."

"That okay, Sid?" Gumby asked, the nickname just coming out naturally.

Sidney nodded. "Of course."

"You think she'll let you pick her up again?" the vet asked.

"Only one way to see." Gumby leaned down and whispered to Hannah, "What do ya say? These nice people are gonna get you all fixed up. Let's not growl at them, okay?"

In response, Hannah lifted her head and licked Gumby's face with a loud slurp.

Everyone chuckled.

"Guess that means she's okay with it." And with that, Gumby once again picked up the large dog and followed the vet into the back area of the animal hospital.

Thirty minutes later, he went back out to the lobby and made a beeline for Sidney. Gumby was somewhat surprised she was still there. A part of him figured she'd bolt the second she was reassured the dog would be taken care of.

He couldn't help but feel a pang of...something... when he saw her waiting for him. It had been a long time since he'd had anyone at his side when he'd had to deal with an emergency like this. Granted, he wouldn't even be dealing with this particular emergency if he hadn't found her fighting on the side of the road, but still.

"Hey," he said softly as he came up beside her and took a seat.

"Hey," she returned, and immediately handed over the clipboard with a piece of paper afixed to it. "I don't know your information."

Gumby stared down at the paper. She'd filled in the information she knew about Hannah, but the top part, where his address and phone number should go, was blank. He couldn't help but notice that her handwriting was beautiful. Neat and precise, nothing like his own.

As he turned his attention to completing the form, she said, "The vet tech asked if I was okay the second you were out of the room."

He looked at her. "What?"

"She wanted to know if I was safe, if I felt uneasy or threatened."

Gumby's fingers tightened on the pen he was holding. "She thought *I* hurt you?"

"Don't look so surprised," she said with a small laugh. "My lip is bleeding, my shirt is torn, and you're one hell of a big guy."

"I would *never* hurt you," Gumby said in a low, intense voice. He looked her in the eye. "I don't hurt women, children, or animals."

The smile left her face and she stared back at him just as intently. "But you do hurt men?"

He shrugged. "If they deserve it. Yes."

Surprised that she didn't ask for an in-depth explanation of what he meant, she only nodded and said, "I told her that we had to chase the guy who took Hannah. That I fell when I was running and busted my lip, and my shirt tore when we had to climb a fence. I don't think she bought it, but there wasn't much she could do if I said I was fine and that you hadn't hurt me."

Gumby brought his hand up to her face and gently ran his thumb over her bottom lip, where it had split in her earlier fight. "Are you really okay?"

"I'm okay," she whispered.

"Decker Kincade?" a loud voice asked from behind them, startling both Gumby and Sidney.

"Here," he said, turning to look at the recep-tionist who'd called his name.

"Just making sure you hadn't left," the woman

said with a sheepish smile. "Take your time with those forms."

Gumby nodded and turned back to Sidney. "I'm about done here. I appreciate your help today."

"That's my line," she returned.

"You gonna give me your phone number so I can keep you updated on Hannah's recovery?" he asked.

She blinked, then retorted, "I think you have it backward. I think you should give me *your* number so I can keep *you* updated on her recovery."

"If you wanted my number, all you had to do was ask, Sid," Gumby teased.

She didn't smile. "I'm serious, Decker."

The grin slid off his face. "Hannah is mine," he told her quietly.

"That makes no sense," Sidney argued. "You can't tell me you had any intention of getting a dog before you found me. You can't make a decision like this at the drop of a hat."

"Come on," he said, standing, grabbing hold of her hand with one of his and pulling her to her feet.

"Decker! What are you—"

"Here are the forms," Gumby told the receptionist as he handed the clipboard to her. "I still need to fill out my personal info, but I'll be right back to complete them." And with that, he towed Sidney out the doors and toward his truck.

Somewhat surprised when she didn't fight him, he stopped next to his truck. After he let go of her hand, Sidney crossed her arms over her chest and glared at him. Except, since she was only around five-two, it wasn't very effective if she was trying to intimidate him.

"I had every intention of getting a dog," he informed her, easily picking up where their conversation had stopped in the waiting area. "I own my own house, so I don't have to worry about any bullshit restrictions when it comes to what kind of dog I can have. I have a good job and I make plenty of money, so I can afford to feed her and make sure she stays healthy. I'm a good guy, Sidney. Why are you so opposed to me adopting her?"

He watched as the bravado slipped away and she sighed. Her arms dropped and her shoulders slumped. "I don't know you. I just met you a little bit ago. This isn't how adoptions work."

"Look at me." When her eyes met his, he said, "I'm gonna take good care of Hannah. She's gonna be spoiled rotten. I'll make a donation to the rescue group if that's what's bothering you."

"It's not the money," she protested. "We do background checks. Make sure adopters are the right fit for a pit bull."

"So do your background check," Gumby told her, confident she wouldn't find anything that would make her or anyone else at the rescue group feel like he wouldn't be a good dog parent.

"Really?" she asked skeptically.

"Really."

She gave him a skeptical look. "Most people don't like it when we tell them about the background check."

"I'm not most people," Gumby said, leaning toward Sidney as he said it.

Neither moved. Their faces were very close, and all he'd have to do is lean down a little bit more and he could take her lips with his own.

The thought was startling. He hadn't been interested in a woman in months. No, at least a year and a half...

Had it really been that long? Gumby tried to remember the last woman he'd gone out with...and couldn't.

But this battered, prickly, and confusing woman made him yearn for something he wasn't sure he could handle. With his job, he hadn't had the best luck when it came to women. His teammate, Rocco, might've found a woman who could deal with the fact he was a Navy SEAL, but it wasn't an easy thing. He was gone a lot, his job was dangerous, and he couldn't exactly tell a girlfriend or wife where he was going or even when he'd be back.

It would be hard enough to have a dog. A woman would complicate his life way more than a pet would.

So why couldn't he stop thinking about how Sidney Hale would taste? How easy it would be to lean down and cover her lips with his own? How she would look sitting in a chair on his back deck, watching the sun set over the ocean as they drank a glass of wine and watched Hannah frolicking in the sand nearby?

It was crazy.

But one thing Gumby had learned from being on the team was that he had to be flexible and go with the flow. Hell, it was one the reasons he'd gotten his nickname. He'd always been that way. Never got ruffled with the curve balls life threw his way.

The team had also started calling him Gumby because one day, when they were in Survival, Evasion, Resistance, and Escape training, he'd been the only one of the six who'd been able to contort his limbs in order to break loose from his bindings.

"Now, will you please give me your number?" he asked.

"So you can let me know how Hannah's doing?" she asked.

"That too."

Her brows furrowed.

"And so I can call you and ask you out."

She blinked. "Well, that's forward."

"Yup."

"Let me guess, women never turn you down and fall at your feet," she said, exasperated.

"Actually," Gumby told her, stepping back, giving her space, "I haven't asked a woman out in longer than I can remember. I haven't been interested in anyone...until now."

"Why me?"

The second the question was out there, Gumby could tell Sidney wanted to take it back.

"Why you?" Gumby asked. "Because it's been a long time since a woman has impressed the hell out of me. I thought I was saving you from a beating, when in reality, you were doing just fine without me. The last thing I expected was for the fight to be over a dog. I'm fascinated by you. I want to know more."

"Oh."

She didn't say anything else, and Gumby

frowned. Shit, she wasn't interested. He'd made a fool out of himself.

"Sorry," he said softly. "It's obviously been so long since I've done this that I'm losing my touch. I wasn't kidding about letting you do that background check though. I'm happy to do whatever adopters usually do so I can officially make Hannah mine."

Sidney put her hand on his forearm, and the skin-on-skin contact was oddly electrifying. She removed her hand almost as soon as she'd touched him, as if she felt the arc of connection between them just as he did. "I wouldn't mind if you called me," she said, then bit her lip. "I just...I'm not sure we're in the same league."

Gumby frowned again. "I don't think I want to know what you mean by that."

"I mean that you have your own house. That's impressive in California because real estate isn't cheap. And I live in a trailer that's seen better days. I don't have a college degree and do work for the trailer park on a part-time basis. You look like the kind of guy who has a perfect family, a perfect house, a kick-ass job, and you were probably voted most likely to succeed in your senior year of high school."

"Most likely to turn up dead before his twenty-first birthday, actually," Gumby told her.

It was Sidney's turn to frown.

"I don't give a shit where you live or that you haven't been to college. I know a lot of assholes who have a university degree who didn't learn a damn thing while they were there. I have never judged anyone by where they live, what job they do, or anything other than the kind of person they are. And from what I've seen in the time I've known you, I have nothing to fear from that quarter. If you just don't want to get to know me, fine, I'm not going to freak out or turn into some obsessed, scorned suiter. Just tell me. Don't make excuses."

Sidney stared at him a long moment before reaching behind her and taking out her phone. "Number?" she asked quietly.

Inwardly sighing in relief, Gumby gave it to her. He felt his phone vibrate in his own pocket, but didn't bother to take it out. "Thank you," he said. "I'll call you as soon as I hear from the vet later on today. She told me that Hannah would probably need to stay here for a bit, until the worst of her wounds heal. Then I can take her home."

"Okay."

"And, even though it might hurt my chances with

you and your rescue organization, I have to admit that I don't know a hell of a lot about dogs. Will you help me?"

"You're really serious about keeping her?"

"Yes."

"Then I'll help you."

"Thank you." He turned to look back at the building before returning his gaze to hers. "Now, I have to go in there and convince them I'm not beating you and that I'm perfectly harmless."

Sidney smiled. "I did see one or two employees peek out the window, probably making sure you weren't smacking me around out here."

Gumby's lips didn't even twitch. "Not funny."

Sidney rolled her eyes. "I need to get home and clean up anyway. I'm sure my boss has a list a mile long of things I need to work on this afternoon."

Gumby nodded and reached up toward her face. She didn't flinch away, not that she could go far with her back up against his truck. He gently brushed his thumb against the black mark forming under her eye. "Get some ice on that to try to stop some of the bruising."

"I will."

Forcing himself to step away from her, Gumby backed toward the building. "Drive safe."

"You too."

Then he turned and quickly strode for the doors to the veterinarian's office once more. With one hand on the door handle, he turned and watched as Sidney pulled out of the parking lot and merged into traffic.

Feeling as if his life had just made a one-eighty, Gumby couldn't stop himself from smiling as he made his way back inside to arrange payment and to make sure his information was on file for later.

Sidney might not think they were in the same league, and she'd be right. Gumby had a feeling she was so far above him it wasn't even funny. But he wasn't going to let her go without a fight. It had been so long since he'd felt even the smallest desire to get to know a woman like he wanted to know Sidney. She'd surprised and impressed him, and that was damn hard to do.

Just wait until he told his teammates that he'd gone from the quintessential bachelor to being a doggy dad—and maybe even being officially off the market—all over his lunch break.

CHAPTER TWO

Later that afternoon, Sidney lay under a double wide trailer as she messed with a leaky water pipe. She thought about everything that had happened earlier, and it almost seemed as if it had happened to someone else.

She'd gotten very used to her life. It had a sameness that was, in many ways, comfortable. Not every exciting, but comfortable. How she'd ended up being a dog rescuer, she didn't know. It wasn't as if she'd planned it. But with her upbringing, she couldn't say she was that surprised.

"Hey, Sid! You under there?" a voice called out.

Smiling, Sidney said, "Yeah! Gimmie a second!" She finished tightening the connection and hoped that would fix the issue. If not, they'd have to replace the entire line, something she knew Jude would be pissed about.

Jude Camara was her boss and the owner of the trailer park. He was in his early sixties, but looked more like he was in his forties. He was big, buff, and tattooed. He'd given her a break when she'd first arrived in California, and Sidney owed him more than she could ever repay. Not in actual money, but because of all the help he'd given her over the years...including paying her to be the park's handy-woman. She'd learned everything she knew about plumbing, electricity, and basic home care from Jude.

Sidney crawled out from under the trailer and looked up at her neighbor. Nora was also thirty-two, but that's where the similarities between them ended. She was tall to Sidney's short. Had beautiful blonde hair to Sidney's dark. She was slender and proportional, and Sidney always felt dumpy and unsophisticated next to her. But Sidney also felt as if she had way more street smarts than Nora. The other woman was constantly jumping from one guy to the next, sure that each would be her ticket out of the trailer park.

Today, Nora was wearing a pair of jeans she looked like she'd been poured into, and a halter top that seemed as if it was one strong gust of wind away from exposing her boobs to the world. Her hair was extra teased and tall, and she'd done her makeup with a heavy hand.

"Hey, Nora," Sidney said as she stood and wiped dirt off her jeans. "What's up?"

"Jeez. What happened to your face?" Nora asked.

Sidney brushed off her concern. "Smacked it on the bottom of one of the trailers."

"Ouch. Anyway, I need your help."

Sidney wasn't surprised. Nora always needed help with something.

"I'm heading out to meet a guy I met on Tinder and was wondering if you'd be my wingman."

"Of course. You want me to text and if things aren't going well, you can pretend to have an emergency so you can leave?" Sidney asked.

Nora laughed. "Oh no. Things are going to go well, I have no doubt about that."

"How do you know?"

Instead of answering, Nora pulled out her phone and clicked a few things before turning it so Sidney could see the picture she'd pulled up.

"That's how I know," Nora said with a smirk.

The guy on the screen was hot, there was no doubt. He was sitting on a Harley-Davidson and smirking. He wore a black muscle shirt that showed off his muscular and tattooed arms, but there was nothing about him that appealed to Sidney. It was as if the man was trying too hard. He was nothing like Decker.

That thought stopped Sidney in her tracks.

What in the world was she doing, comparing this guy to Decker? It was crazy. She'd just met the man today.

"He's good-looking," Sidney told her friend with a smile, trying to push thoughts of Decker Kincade to the back of her mind.

"Good-looking?" Nora asked in disbelief. "He's fucking *hot*. And I'm going to be in his bed this afternoon if it's the last thing I do."

Sidney chuckled and shook her head. Nora was nothing if not optimistic. "What do you need my help with then?"

"I told him that I had a roommate," Nora said. "I need you to call in about an hour and half, and I'm going to pretend that you told me we had a water pipe burst so I can't go home. I'll milk it so he'll feel sorry for me and let me stay at his place. Then I'll blow his...*mind*...so skillfully, he won't want me to leave anytime soon!"

Sidney didn't understand her friend's desire to

sleep with half the male population, but she didn't look down at her for it either. Nora definitely had the body to go with her sex drive. "You think he'll fall for it?"

"Oh yeah," Nora said. "He's gonna take one look at this," she gestured to herself with one hand, "and fall over backward to get it."

"What does he do?" Sidney asked.

Nora shrugged. "No clue."

"Where's he from?"

Again Nora shrugged. "Here, I guess."

Sidney shook her head in exasperation. "Do you know anything about him at *all*?"

"I know he's got a Prince Albert and a big dick."

Sidney rolled her eyes. "I don't want to know how you know *that*, but you have no idea what he does for a living."

Nora smirked. "He sent me a picture, of course."

"Gross," Sidney said, wrinkling her nose.

"Oh honey. We need to get you laid," Nora said sympathetically. "Because his Johnson definitely isn't gross. Not at all."

"I'm good, thanks," Sidney told her. "You have a condom?"

"A whole box, thanks, Mom," Nora said with a roll of her eyes.

"Good. And if you need me to rescue you because it turns out the picture he used on Tinder isn't really him, and he's actually an accountant who wears glasses, a pocket protector, and highwater pants, just call me. I'll go with the flow and say whatever you need me to in order to get you out of there."

"Sid, I don't care in the least if it's not him in the picture, as long as the picture he sent of his dick is the real thing. It's been a week and a half since I've gotten me some, and I'm due."

That was the other thing Sidney didn't understand. It had been three *years* since she'd slept with anyone and, frankly, her vibrator gave her three times the pleasure any man ever had. She didn't get the hype.

"Okay. You go and have fun. I'll call in a bit," Sidney told her.

"Thanks. You're a gem," Nora told her, then leaned forward and gave her an air kiss.

Sidney returned the gesture and watched as Nora strutted off. She had on a pair of four-inch heels and didn't seem to be fazed by the fact she was walking on uneven, rocky ground.

Looking down at herself, Sidney grimaced. She was covered in dirt from head to toe, and the one time she'd tried to walk in heels, she'd fallen flat on her face.

In many ways, she admired Nora. She didn't care that she used her body and face to get men to pay for shit for her. She didn't have a job, but didn't need one because she constantly had men "loaning" her money. She wasn't a whore, didn't take money to sleep with men, but *because* she slept with them, they gave it to her. It was a thin line, but Sidney was the last person who would ever judge Nora.

She was kind, would happily share her last dollar if someone needed it, and always had a smile on her face. Yeah, Sidney liked her, and even envied her sometimes. She also had a great relationship with her family—something Sidney had never had.

Refusing to think about her family, knowing it would just lead her down a road she didn't want to go, Sidney was about to grab her tool bag to head to the next job she had to get done when her phone vibrated in her pocket.

Pulling it out, she saw Decker's name on the screen.

Feeling suddenly giddy, she considered letting the call go to voice mail. But she was too curious about Hannah to do that.

"Hello?"

"Hey, Sidney. It's Decker."

"Hi."

"I wanted to call and let you know the doc called me back. Hannah's wounds looked worse than they were. She agreed with our assessment that she was dragged behind a car, which ripped out all her toenails and basically burned the pads off her feet. Those'll be wrapped up for a while so they can heal."

"And her back?"

"Her best guess is battery acid."

"God. People are such assholes," Sidney breathed.

"Yeah. Totally in agreement with you there. She cleaned her back and said the hair probably wouldn't grow back, but the damage wasn't as bad as it might've been if she hadn't gotten medical care so quickly. Apparently Hannah looks funny with half her back shaved, but she reassured me that the hair'll grow back quickly around the burn."

"Good. How long will they have to keep her?"

"She said probably only about a week or so. A lot depends on how she does once she wakes up."

"Right. I can call Faith, the lady who runs the pit bull rescue I've been working with, and she can pay for Hannah's treatment," Sidney told Decker.

"Nope. I got it. Just give me her number, and I'll call her and get the ball rolling on adopting Hannah."

Sidney bit her lip. "I haven't told her about Hannah yet."

Sidney was almost as surprised as Decker seemed to be, if his silence was any indication. Usually calling the president of the rescue group was the first thing she did after getting her hands on a pit bull. But for some reason, she hadn't this time. Some of it was because she'd once again broken the law in order to get Hannah out of that asshole's clutches.

But mostly it was because of Decker.

"You know I'm willing to do whatever's necessary in order to adopt her," Decker said after a moment.

"I know. But it seems as if it's just a lot of unnecessary red tape at this point. You want her. She likes you. Making you pay the adoption fee on top of what you're already paying the vet doesn't seem right."

"I feel kinda like a little kid whose mom just pushed him up on the diving board and told him to jump," Decker said with a laugh. "Will you help me figure out what I need to get for— Oh...shit."

"What?" Sidney asked, alarmed.

"My house. I'm in the middle of renovating it. There's shit everywhere. I can't bring a dog here."

"It can't be that bad," Sidney said. When Decker didn't respond, she winced. "*Is* it that bad?"

"I just...I live alone. And spend most of my time on my back deck. I haven't been in any hurry to get the house done. I bought it as a foreclosure and it needed a lot of work. Both inside and outside. But I got it for a steal. I figured I had boatloads of time."

"Do you want me to come over and take a look? I'm pretty handy."

The offer popped out before Sidney even thought about what she was saying. She bit her lip and closed her eyes. Shit, Decker was going to think she was totally coming on to him. He'd think she was easy, and probably take advantage.

"Seriously?"

Sidney opened her eyes and stared blankly at the side of the trailer she'd just been under. "Yeah."

"I'd love that." He sounded relieved.

"I'm sure a professional contractor would probably be a better bet," she told him honestly, trying to backtrack.

"I've got a contractor, but you're the dog expert. If you're serious, you can help me figure out what needs to be done immediately so Hannah will be safe here. Then I can call Max and get that done, and work on the smaller shit when time permits."

"Okay."

"How about tomorrow?"

"Tomorrow?" Sidney asked in surprise.

"Yeah. I don't have a lot of time, not if Hannah is going to be released within the week," Decker told her.

"Right." Of course that's why he wanted her to come over so quickly.

"That, and I want to see you again," he added.

Swallowing hard, Sidney did her best to keep the butterflies in her stomach under control. It had been a long time since she'd felt this way about anything. Especially a man.

And Decker was one hell of a man. She'd noticed that he was good-looking, of course she had, but it wasn't until Hannah had been taken to the back at the vet's that she'd really had time to reflect.

The T-shirt he'd had on pulled tight over his shoulders and biceps, showing off how buff he was. He had tattoos on his arms down to his wrists, all black, which was hot as hell. He also had a fairly full, neatly trimmed beard, which intrigued Sidney. She'd never dated a man with a beard before, and couldn't deny she was curious as to how it might feel to kiss him. Would the hair on his face be scratchy and annoying? Or would it be soft and tickle as his lips covered her own?

She closed her eyes and tried to get her mind back on track. She wasn't like Nora, didn't expect sex in return for doing him a favor, but she had a feeling a naked Decker would be absolutely beautiful—and almost overwhelming, next to her less-than-perfect figure.

"What time?" she asked, trying to get her mind out of the gutter.

"Whatever time is good for you," he returned immediately.

"Don't you have to work?" she asked, suddenly wondering what it was he did for a living. He'd certainly had time that afternoon to help her and take Hannah to the vet. He said he had a job, but maybe that was a lie. Maybe he *didn't* work. Maybe he was a trust fund kid and lived off his parents' money...

"Yeah. But at the moment, my time is flexible. It's not always this way, but I might as well take advantage of it while I can."

She wanted to ask about his job, *so* bad, but decided it would sound rude. She'd ask tomorrow.

"Okay. How about two-ish? I need to help Jude out in the morning since I was gone most of today."

"Jude?" Decker asked.

Sidney thought she heard a note of jealousy in his tone, but that was crazy. "My boss."

"Hmmm."

"My sixty-three-year-old boss," she added, wanting to make sure he knew she wasn't in any way attracted to the other man.

"Right. I was that obvious, huh?" Decker said with a laugh. "Thank you for not playing games, Sid. Two sounds perfect. Do you want me to pick you up?"

"What? Why?"

"Because you're doing me a favor by coming to my place to help me. It's the least I could do."

"No. I'll meet you there," she said firmly. There was no way she was going to be trapped at his house without transportation. She'd just met the guy. She wasn't an idiot.

"You can trust me," Decker said, his voice having lowered. "I know how that sounded, but you have nothing to fear from me. To you, I'm harmless."

She noted that he didn't say he was harmless in general. Some wouldn't even note the distinction, but it was more than obvious to her. "I'll come to you." The words sounded innocent in her head, but the second they came out of her lips, they seemed to have a deeper meaning.

"I'll text you my address," Decker said.

"Okay."

"Sidney?"

"Yeah?"

"Thank you."

"You're welcome."

"I'll see you tomorrow."

"Bye."

"Bye."

Sidney clicked off the phone and stared at it unseeingly. It wasn't until it vibrated in her hand that she shook herself out of the stupor she'd been in.

Looking down, she saw Decker had indeed texted his address. She brought it up on the map and inwardly groaned.

Of course he had a house right on the beach.

What was she doing? She hadn't been kidding when she'd said he was way out of her league. Someone like Nora could probably snare him in a second…but then she'd turn her back and walk away without a second glance, as well.

Decker Kincade didn't strike her as a ladies' man. He had a sincerity about him. A goodness.

And she should stay as far away from him as she could get.

She'd taint him. As sure as her name was Sidney Hale, she knew that without a doubt. She should go ahead and tell him who her brother was, get it over with.

But selfishly, she wanted a little more time to just be Sidney. To enjoy the strange connection she had with Decker...

Before he looked at her in horror and found a way to distance himself from her.

Sighing, Sidney shoved her phone back in her pocket and picked up her tool bag. She had shit to do, and thinking about the chocolate-brown eyes of Decker Kincade was not on the list.

**

Pick up *Securing Sidney* NOW!